"Max! You're not listening to me."

"Eleanor, I'm hearing you loud and clear. Now you're not listening to me. I don't do threats. I don't do ultimatums. I have a real opportunity to collect meaningful data that might help people really see what's happening to our planet. I'm sorry but that's more important than four months of our marriage."

"No, Max," she said sadly. "What you mean is that it's more important than me."

"Nor..."

She took a step away. "Stay safe."

"I'll see you in four months."

She shook her head. "No. You won't."

He wrapped a hand around her neck and forced her to hold still for his kiss. Not that he ever had to force her to kiss him. Kissing Max Harper was her own particular addiction.

And this might be their last kiss.

Knowing that, she clung to him. Wrapped her arms around his neck and gave him everything that she was. Everything that she ever would be.

Until finally she couldn't take it anymore and she pulled away.

When she did, she was crying. "I love you, Max Harper."

"I know. Which is how I know I'll see you in four months."

Dear Reader,

Does anyone remember the TV show *General Hospital*? I used to love soap operas growing up as a kid. There was always that favorite character who "died"...which really meant he or she tried to get a job in a movie or a nighttime TV show. If that didn't happen, he or she could always miraculously return in dramatic fashion as undead.

That germ was the basis for Max and Eleanor. A couple who truly loved each other, but it wasn't enough to keep them together. However, when something life changing happens, it's easy to see how priorities can shift.

I hope you root for this couple as much as I did while writing them.

I love to hear from readers, so you can find me at stephaniedoyle.net.

Stephanie

STEPHANIE DOYLE

Married...Again

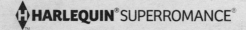
HARLEQUIN® SUPERROMANCE®

Recycling programs for this product may not exist in your area.

ISBN-13: 978-1-335-44910-8

Married...Again

Copyright © 2018 by Stephanie Doyle

Printed in U.S.A.

Stephanie Doyle, a dedicated romance reader, began to pen her own romantic adventures at age sixteen. She began submitting to Harlequin at age eighteen and by twenty-six her first book was published. Fifteen years later, she still loves what she does, as each book is a new adventure. She lives in South Jersey with her cat, Hermione, the designated princess of the house. When Stephanie's not reading or writing, in the summer she is most likely watching a baseball game and eating a hot dog.

Books by Stephanie Doyle

HARLEQUIN SUPERROMANCE

Her Secret Service Agent

The Bakers of Baseball

The Comeback of Roy Walker
Scout's Honor
Betting on the Rookie

The Way Back
One Final Step
An Act of Persuasion

For the First Time
Remembering That Night

HARLEQUIN ROMANTIC SUSPENSE

Suspect Lover
The Doctor's Deadly Affair

SILHOUETTE BOMBSHELL

Calculated Risk
The Contestant
Possessed

Visit the Author Profile page at Harlequin.com for more titles.

CHAPTER ONE

Trondheim Research Facility, Norway

"I CAN'T BELIEVE you right now," Eleanor Harper shouted at her husband even as he walked down the stairs away from her.

"Nor, I'm not going to have this fight," he said over his shoulder.

"No! No! You are going to have this fight. We are going to have this fight. Max, stop!"

He stopped at the door, his packed duffel bag slung over his shoulder. He turned to her, and she could see it in his expression. Before he even opened his mouth, she knew that he wasn't going to back down.

That all the yelling and pleading and begging in the world wasn't going to change this.

He huffed. "Nor! This is who I am. This is what I do. Do you get that? I'm an oceanographer who studies the impact of climate change on the ocean. This planet is dying one damn inch at a time. I *have* to do this work now. We've talked about this before. I thought I had your support."

That wasn't fair. This wasn't about her not supporting his work. "You do have my support. You have all the support a wife should give to her husband, but where is *my* support? You dragged me to this research facility, and I said fine. I'll go where you go. No questions asked. Then as soon as we get here you're turning around and leaving me. For months at a time. I have no friends here, no family."

Max rolled his eyes. "Oh, please, Nor, don't sit there and tell me you're pining away for your mother."

"That's not the point. Like it or not, she's my mother. I miss my family. My sister. I miss my life back home. And none of that would matter if I had you. But now you tell me you're leaving me again. Not for three months this time, but *four* months. That's almost half of a year. I'm supposed to just sit around here and wait for you?"

Eleanor watched as he dropped the duffel on the floor beside him. Maybe she was getting through to him.

"It's not fair, Max. It's not, and you can't tell me otherwise."

He walked toward her and put his hands on her shoulders, pressed his forehead to hers.

So close she could smell him. She loved the scent of him. No matter how long he'd been on shore, to her he always smelled like the ocean.

"Nor, look at me. There are times you have to accept that some things are bigger than any one person. Bigger than any one relationship. Four months is nothing to us. A blip in our life."

She shook her head and stepped out of his reach. "No, it's four months this time. Then five months the next time. Then a year after that. It's always going to be you needing to be on the ocean finding more and more data. Thinking you can prove that climate change is happening and suddenly everyone will listen to you."

"Yes, Nor. The data I collect. It's important. Not just for me but for everyone on this planet."

"You have to make a choice. You have to choose. A life with me or a life on the ocean. But you can't have both."

He frowned. "Ultimatums? You're sitting

there, right now, issuing me an ultimatum. How crappy is that?"

Eleanor could feel tears welling up, but she worked hard to make sure her voice didn't crack when she said it. "Max, do you love me?"

"With everything I am."

She smiled sadly. Because it was true. It's what she felt every day. But only when he was here. Only when he was with her. They had dated a mere seven months before he proposed. Before she accepted. Her mother had thought the proposal had come too soon. So much so that she refused to put together any kind of wedding until the two of them came to their senses and waited at least a year.

Giving Eleanor no option other than the obvious one. They'd eloped. To this day, almost three years later, her mother was still furious about it.

"We've been married nearly three years, and in that time we've only been together eighteen months. I can't...I can't...keep doing this."

"Well, maybe it's time you thought about your own passions."

It felt like a slap of some kind. "What?"

"Look, I know it's hard when I'm gone. It's

hard for me, too. You think I like spending my days with a bunch of other smelly scientists and rough sailors on the freezing cold Arctic Ocean? I like spending my days with you. I like spending my nights with my wife. I like screwing my wife. I wouldn't do this if I didn't think it was vitally important. So while I'm gone, maybe you need to find that thing, too. The thing you think is important."

"I think you're important," Eleanor told him. Not sure why he was saying what he was saying.

"Nor, I can't be the only thing in your life. That is not the woman I married. You're not this clingy weak thing. You are Eleanor Gaffney. You're the girl who shook off her small Nebraska town, who found a way to put herself through school. You were going to rule the world. What happened to that girl?"

You married her and took her to a research facility in northern Norway. Eleanor wanted to say those things, but it sounded pathetic in her own head. Then she did the only thing she could think of, the thing they had both talked about having.

"We talked about getting pregnant this year," she said.

Another snort. "Really? You're pulling the baby card?"

The sound of his disbelief made her furious. "A baby is not a *card*. It's supposed to be about having family. It's what we both talked about wanting. We talked about doing it this year!"

"Are you pregnant now?"

"No," she told him.

"Then when I get back in four months, we'll talk about this. But I mean it, Nor, you need to find out what you want to do with yourself, with your life. Because being my wife, and hell, being the mother to our future children, isn't enough. You need something for you."

"I studied business! What the hell am I supposed to do with that in Trondheim? Create an ice-selling business? Oh, I know! What about a new pickled herring recipe?"

He had the audacity to smile at her. "Are you going to kiss me goodbye? I'm running late as it is."

Eleanor shook her head as it finally settled on her. The truth. He was leaving. He was leaving, and his answer to that was she needed to find a hobby that would occupy her time while he was away.

This was going to be her life. Watching him leave and waiting for him to come back. She hadn't known that's what it would be when she married him. She didn't know that going in or she would have...

You would have married him anyway. Your mother was right. You're too stubborn for your own good.

"I don't think you understand what I've been trying to tell you. If you leave me, I'm leaving you."

Eleanor watched as his whole body tensed.

Max shook his head. "You don't mean it."

"Look at me, Max." Eleanor stood in front of him, and she knew in her heart she meant every word she said. It would take all her courage to leave him, but she would do it. "I love you. Like no one I've ever loved before. But I can't spend my life doing this. Watching you leave. So it might break me, but if you leave, then I'm gone."

"I'm not going to be brought to heel by my wife," he snapped. "I'm not your damn dog."

"I'm not trying to do that. I'm trying to save our marriage. You think love is enough."

"It should be," he shouted.

"It's not. It's about compromise and working together and finding a solution. It's not about you telling me the day before, *Sorry, babe, I need to leave for a while*, and that while is four months."

"The funding came though from Tom yesterday. I had no control over that. Or when the ship leaves. I told you that, too."

"Max! You're not listening to me."

"Eleanor, I'm hearing you loud and clear. Now you're not listening to me. I don't do threats. I don't do ultimatums. I have a real opportunity to collect meaningful data that might help people really see what's happening to our planet. I'm sorry, but that's more important than four months of our marriage."

She swallowed as the words penetrated her skull. "No, Max," she said sadly. "What you mean is that it's more important than me."

"Nor..."

She took a step away. "Stay safe."

"I'll see you in four months."

She shook her head. "No. You won't."

He wrapped a hand around her neck and forced her to hold still for his kiss. Not that he ever had to force her to kiss him. Kissing Max Harper was her own particular addiction.

And this might be their last kiss.

Knowing that, she clung to him. Wrapped her arms around his neck and gave him everything that she was. Everything that she ever would be.

Until finally she couldn't take it anymore and she pulled away.

When she did, she was crying. "I love you, Max Harper."

"I know. Which is how I know I'll see you in four months."

Four months later

HE HADN'T BELIEVED HER. When she said she would leave him, he just couldn't believe she would do it. They loved each other. Sometimes almost too much. It was a scary thing to know how vulnerable you were when you loved someone that much.

Which was why he hadn't believed her when she said she would leave him.

Except the empty house told its own story. So did the people they were renting it from.

Mrs. Harper had left months ago. Right after he left on his trip.

The only thing waiting for him was a large brown envelope with the name of an attorney's office in the upper left corner.

He wasn't going to open it. He wasn't going to see what she chose to throw away. He was going to do what he needed to do, then he was going after her.

He'd come home with a sick feeling of dread in his stomach. Not because he even entertained the idea that she would leave him. He looked at his life, his work as if he was at war. Against time, against the forces of nature and the forces of mankind. He was a soldier, and their marriage was like any other military marriage. One where he would need to be deployed from time to time.

So the feeling of dread he'd felt coming home was knowing he would have to tell her that he was turning around and heading out in a few weeks. The financing for yet another extension had come through.

He'd expected more shouting, more fighting. He'd thought he could power through all of that with some mind-blowing sex that would remind her of what they had. How incendiary they could be.

He'd thought wrong.

It didn't matter. Max stared at the brown envelope with his name on it, then dumped it in the trash, unopened.

He would fix this. He would head out to sea for just a few more weeks, finish what he needed to finish, then he would go find her. Because there was no world he could live in where they weren't together.

Nor was angry. She was hurt. He knew that. But he also knew he could fix both those things. One more trip, then they could move forward with their life together.

Three months later

"SELENA?" ELEANOR CALLED to her assistant. Selena had been the first official employee of Head to Toe, Eleanor's start-up company. "The red or burgundy?"

Eleanor held the ties against the mannequin's neck.

Selena assessed the outfit, then nodded. "The red."

"I agree."

The two were working in the space Eleanor had recently rented. It was an open loft area in downtown Denver that would be perfect as they continued to expand. Running Head to Toe out of her apartment just wasn't practical anymore.

The business was a simple concept directed at busy single men. Head to Toe put together a complete outfit that would fit whatever need those men had. An outfit composed by women who knew what they were doing.

Don't have a woman in your life who can tell you what tie to wear? What color looks best on you? That, no, that belt and those shoes don't match. Try Head to Toe!

It had been the banner that ran along the top of the website, and, with the help of some targeted Facebook ads, orders had started to pour in. Business casual, formal, club scene and even the local bar look. They told Eleanor what they liked to wear, how they wanted to look, and Eleanor put together the perfect outfit for them. As the orders continued to come, she spent more time focusing on advertising. Now her market research was generating real results.

So much that, beyond the warehouse people she'd hired to handle shipping and Selena—whom she had hired a few months ago to help keep up with orders—Eleanor was now looking to expand further with a dedicated client service support team.

Which meant filling the loft with office furniture and computers.

A sign on the door.

Actually, she needed the door first.

It had become what felt like a 24/7 effort on her part, but she didn't mind the work. Watching something grow under her efforts was one of the most satisfying things she'd ever done.

Beyond that, the constant workload stopped her from thinking about Max.

Most days.

She heard a hesitant knock on the doorframe, which outlined the entrance to the space. Eleanor assumed it was her next interview. She was looking for someone with experience who could help her grow both a design team as well as a customer service department.

While there were men out there who had no

problem navigating the online site, some men had a harder time using the tools provided to get a sense of what their own personal style was.

They liked talking directly to Eleanor and Selena, but quite frankly, neither could keep up with the phone calls any longer.

Eleanor peeked around the mannequin, startled to find Harry. Her former father-in-law.

Or more accurately current father-in-law as Max had yet to sign the divorce papers. Eleanor assumed he was being stubborn, but she couldn't imagine how that was supposed to be a strategy for him.

Any hope she'd had about their marriage had gone out the door when four months after she left him ticked by on her calendar and she hadn't heard from him. Not even an irate call at some off hour because he'd be phoning her from Norway to tell her to go eff herself.

Instead, there had been only silence. Which hurt more than anything. Because it told her, more than all of his professions of love, that leaving her had been too easy for him. Where for her, if it hadn't been for her idea for this business, she might have crawled into a hole and stayed there forever.

Maybe Harry had come as an envoy. With the papers. To put an end to the marriage finally.

Eleanor walked through the open loft to meet him. She'd seen both him and Sarah when she'd gotten back. She'd considered them her family, and it had been almost as devastating to tell them she was leaving as it had been actually leaving Max.

She knew they didn't understand. She knew she'd hurt them. But Max had left her with no options.

"Hello, Harry."

"Nor," he said, using Max's nickname for her. Max had always felt *Eleanor* was too regal, and since he was no damn king, he liked to call her by a name that was his and his alone.

It hurt, she thought. Even after all this time. Eleanor had lost her own father when she was just eighteen. Having Harry in her life had filled a hole that had been empty. Divorcing Max had brought back even that pain. The pain of not having that father figure in her world, who was always there with a ready hug to tell her everything was going to be okay.

"How is Sarah?"

He didn't look good, Eleanor thought. He looked older than she remembered when it had been only a few months since she'd last seen him. Suddenly now, she was worried. Was someone sick?

"I don't know how to tell you this," he said gruffly. "So I'm just going to come out and say it. Max is…Max is gone."

"Gone? What do you mean? Off on another assignment? I suppose I assumed that."

Harry shook his head. "No. After he got back from the last assignment, he called us to tell us what happened with you two. We told him you had been by to see us and explain. He said they had gotten additional funding, and he was going to do another month at sea. That as soon as he got back he was going to come home to the States and fix things between you two. I told him he should do that now. I told him how serious you seemed about the whole thing. That you had said you wanted a divorce. But you know how stubborn he can be."

She did. She knew exactly how stubborn he could be.

"The ship…it's gone. They think it went down in a storm. They've been looking for weeks and weeks. But there is no communication and no sign of it on any radar. I just got a call from the university today. They told us at this point we have to assume there were no survivors."

He stopped talking, and Eleanor took a second to process what he was saying.

Max was on a ship. The ship was gone. There were no survivors.

Max was dead.

It was the strangest thing she ever did, but she laughed. Actually laughed at her husband's grieving father. She reached out and gently touched him on the arm.

"Oh, Harry, Max isn't dead. He can't be."

She would know it if he was dead. She would feel it. Her plan in life was to hate Max Harper every day from now until the day she died. A lifetime of hating him for not putting her first. For not choosing correctly when he had a choice between his work or her.

A lifetime of it.

He couldn't be dead.

"I'm sorry, sweetie. I know things didn't end well between you two. Sarah and I were both so sad about that."

"He's not dead, Harry. I would know it."

He nodded. "Sarah says the same. But we can only go by what the experts are telling us, and they have officially declared him dead. We're going to hold a service, and we would appreciate it if you were there. No matter how you two ended, you were family. His and ours for a time."

Harry patted her hand, then turned to leave. Eleanor shook her head, still not understanding what had happened. There was no way this could be right. No way she was going to lose Max.

Again.

She stumbled back to her desk in the center of the loft and pulled up her laptop.

"Eleanor? Everything okay?"

She ignored her assistant while she typed Max Harper Oceanographer in a Google search page.

And there it was on her screen.

Max Harper, renowned oceanographer and

climate scientist, declared dead along with the crew of the ship the *Savior*.

She fell to her knees, and Selena immediately crouched on the floor next to her.

"Eleanor, what's wrong? What's the matter? Are you sick?"

No, she thought. *I'm not sick. I'm dead.*

CHAPTER TWO

Two and a half years later

"A TOAST! To my lovely daughter and her fiancé. I, as I'm sure everyone here does, wish them the most happiness. And I know my dear husband, Frank, is smiling down on them from heaven."

Eleanor looked at her mother in the center of the room and smiled even as she lifted her glass in the air. She glanced at her sister, Allie, and her fiancé, Mike, and was happy to see they seemed to be having a nice time.

The house was filled with family and friends for the engagement party. A party she knew Allie and Mike didn't originally want, hoping to keep things as low-key as possible. They had just announced their engagement last week, and no sooner had that happened than Marilyn was planning the party despite Allie's objections. However, Marilyn was insistent, and, in the Gaffney household, whatever Marilyn wanted, Marilyn got.

Whether her children felt the same or not.

The wedding was almost a year away, but Eleanor had already agreed to take time from her company to make sure she could attend all the various activities. Tonight was just the start. Eventually there would be a bridal shower, then the bachelorette party, the rehearsal dinner, all culminating in what Marilyn Gaffney was proclaiming would be the event of the season in the town of Hartsville, Nebraska, next June.

Given that the population of Hartsville was just a little over five thousand citizens, any wedding that happened in town usually was the event of the season.

"Some champagne?"

Eleanor turned at the sound of the voice behind her. Daniel, her date for the evening, held up two flutes. She gladly accepted one.

"Thank you. You may need to keep this coming."

"You seem to be getting along with your mother," he said in a lowered voice. "From everything you had told me on the drive here, I was expecting something a little more dramatic between you two."

"I'm trying to do everything I can to avoid the drama. Mom and I are fine as long as I'm agreeing with her. It's when I don't that things become difficult. Take this party, for example. Completely unnecessary. We're going to be seeing all these same people at the wedding. What's the point of doing it twice?"

Daniel raised an eyebrow. "What's the point of any party? To have fun."

Eleanor looked at Allie and Mike again. They were still smiling, still chatting with the people around them. They looked like what they were. A couple in love. A couple who was excited about their future.

And Eleanor was happy for them.

All this wedding paraphernalia didn't bother her. Not in the least. That's what she was telling herself anyway, and she could be very convincing when she needed to be.

Still, she knew everything on the surface wasn't always as it appeared.

"I know my sister. It's going to be hard enough for her to be the center of attention for a day. To keep this up for the next year will be laborious. A wedding shouldn't be that much work."

"Speaking of weddings...do you like big ones or small ones? Just so I can get an idea."

"Daniel," she said with a soft sigh.

"I hate that sigh, you know. I was only teasing."

Was he? It was hard to know with Daniel. He liked to call himself a man of action, and that was true. He was always very persistent in getting what he wanted. Much like her mother.

Like convincing her to go out with him when she'd refused him for months.

"This is only our second date. I think it's a little too soon to talk about weddings, don't you?"

He gripped his chest in mock pain. "What? You're not counting all those lunches?"

"They were business lunches," she reminded him.

"One woman's business lunch, another man's date."

"So you're saying you have no real interest in investing in Head to Toe?"

He sipped his champagne. "I wouldn't say that exactly. No."

"That's what I thought," Eleanor said smugly. "Daniel, I agreed to go out with you. I agreed to bring you here so you could meet my family. But you know where my head is right now. Head to Toe is getting bigger every day, and it has to be my number-one priority. I've told you my plans."

"You have. Or you could turn those plans over to me and let them be my number-one priority. Then you could go back to focusing on...other areas of your life."

Again, she thought he was teasing, but it was hard to tell. Their relationship had started when Daniel, an investment banker, had shown interest in the growth rate of her company located in Denver. He'd asked her out to lunch to discuss the idea of what a large cash infusion could mean. She'd rejected the idea at first, but then the idea to get ahead of the game by growing her company at an accelerated rate seemed compelling.

Which led to another lunch.

Which led to her thinking Daniel himself was rather attractive. It might have been the first time in years she had even registered a man's appearance. That had to be a good thing, she told herself.

In the end, Daniel hadn't swayed her with his pitch. Head to Toe was her baby, and a cash investment from someone else meant giving part of it away. Whereas, if she took a loan out for the money to expand, it would still be hers. One was riskier, but the other was tantamount to giving over part control of the business. She didn't know if she was willing to do that.

Daniel, however, had not been willing to walk away, either.

She would have thought his interest was solely in the company until he surprised her on lunch number two by asking her out on a date. Of course, she said no, for any number of reasons. But he persisted until she got to that point where she realized there was absolutely no reason for her not to go out on a date with him.

He was an intelligent, handsome, sometimes funny man. She liked him. A date made sense. A date might make her normal again. Two years was a long time to grieve a marriage that she had chosen to end.

They'd had an elegant dinner. They had agreed not to talk about work.

It had been...nice.

So she'd asked him to come to this party with her. Only now, he was suggesting there was something missing in her life.

"And what areas would those be?"

"I don't know. Maybe thinking about other things than your company. Other things you want in life. You were married once. Don't you think about getting married again?"

Eleanor flinched. "I don't like to talk about my marriage."

Because it was hers. Her marriage. Her memories. And talking about Max...thinking about him hurt too much.

"I can see why this would be painful to discuss..."

"We are at a party," Eleanor said, raising her glass to her lips trying to change the subject. "Didn't you say something about it being fun?"

This time it was Daniel who sighed.

"Eleanor, you have to see that I care about you."

Did she? Did she have to see that? After a bunch of lunches and two dates—the second one not even finished yet. They hadn't even had sex yet. She didn't want to think about how even the idea of sex with him made her feel.

Disloyal was the best word she could come up with.

"I only want what is best for you. I feel sometimes like I'm battling this ghost."

"You're not."

"We haven't talked about this. I'm not sure I know how you feel about children—"

Eleanor pierced him with a look that stopped that sentence. If she wasn't comfortable talking about her marriage, then she certainly wasn't comfortable discussing the subject of children with Daniel. Definitely not on a second date.

"There you are!" Marilyn proclaimed as she approached them. "You're not mingling. Everyone is asking about you, but it seems no one is getting a chance to talk with you."

For the first time in her life, Eleanor was happy to be admonished by her mother. Anything to get Daniel to stop talking about Max and babies.

"Sorry, Mom. Daniel and I were just having a conversation."

Marilyn smiled and patted his arm. "Yes,

yes. I'm very happy with your new young man, but you two can talk all you want when you're back in the big city. For now, I would like my daughter to be available for her family."

"Yes, of course," Daniel said graciously. "We'll make our way around the room."

"That would be lovely. I do hope it's not too inconvenient that we have you at the B and B in town. I know I'm old-fashioned. However, until a couple is married, I just don't feel comfortable with them sharing a room—"

"Mom." Eleanor had told her mother only that she was bringing someone she was currently seeing. She definitely hadn't gone into detail about their sexual status. "It's fine. Daniel is only staying for tonight. He has to head back to the city tomorrow."

Her mother made a face as if the word *city* was distasteful. Probably because she associated Denver with Eleanor's business, something else she found distasteful. Her mother still clung to the belief that a woman's first priority should be securing a husband and having children.

Eleanor had done half of that and had failed.

Since then she hadn't been eager to repeat the experience.

Her business, however, was a nice replacement. Way less pain and heartbreak. More control and financial benefit. As far as Eleanor was concerned, if she never got married again, it wouldn't be the most tragic thing to happen to her.

Because the most tragic thing had already happened.

Her mother was obviously not pleased by that attitude. It meant fewer grandchildren.

"Oh. Well, let's hope you're still in Eleanor's life for the wedding."

"I promise to do everything I can to make sure I'm back for that. In the meantime, this will be the first weekend Eleanor's been away from her company in some time. I hope she has time for some relaxation."

"Of course it will be relaxing," Marilyn stated, turning to Eleanor. "She'll be with family. Now, speaking of, your father's sister and brother want to talk with you. I suggest you start with them. Since your father's been gone, they claim to feel left out of your and your sister's lives. I'm making every effort to change that with *this* wedding."

Eleanor didn't miss the emphasis on the word *this*. Five years later and she was still being punished for her elopement to Max. One would have thought, considering what she went through with his death, she might have been forgiven.

But her mother had a long memory.

"Yes, Mom. I'll head over to them shortly."

Marilyn left them, and Eleanor could hear her greeting some new guests as they came through the front door.

"She really does love to play the hostess," Daniel noted.

"Yes, she does. Now, if you don't mind, I'm going to make small talk with my family, so they can get as much gossip out of me as possible. Most of them want to know how much money I'm making. Truly, they are not even subtle about it."

Daniel laughed. "I think I'll stand in this corner and drink myself silly. Mike already promised he would drive me to the B and B."

"Yes, poor Mike. He and Allie live together on his farm in North Platte, but now my mother is making him pay for a room. It's so impractical. But Marilyn's house, Marilyn's rules."

"Hmm," Daniel said. "A strong-minded woman. Sounds like someone else I know."

Eleanor gasped. "Are you comparing me to my mother? Daniel Reynolds. That's grounds for murder!"

He laughed again. "I believe you have small talk to make."

"I'm on it."

Eleanor had no problem with mingling. Unlike Allie, Eleanor was used to being the center of attention every day at work. Daniel had been accurate. This really was going to be her first real break from the office since its inception almost three years ago. An office that had started with her, then Selena, now housed an IT staff, a customer service department, an advertising and sales department and a buying department comprised mostly of part-time, stay-at-home moms. Eleanor also had a bookkeeper, but now even Shelly was complaining she needed help to keep up.

Yet another hire. Of course that meant the company was growing, which was a good thing, Eleanor told herself.

The point was she dealt with dozens of people, of varying personalities, all day long. Working a room, making people feel comfortable, listening to them was all part of her daily routine. After an hour of small talk, she managed to find her way to Allie and Mike.

Allie's smile was in place, but Eleanor could see the tension in her shoulders, the strain in her face.

"How are you holding up?" Eleanor asked.

"I'm fine. I'm great. This is amazing."

"Allie, seriously? This is me you're talking to."

"Seriously. I figured out the best way to get through all of this is just to accept it. Mom wanted a party. Mom gets a party. Then in less than a year, after the actual wedding, all of this will be over."

Eleanor could feel the anger rising. "Allie, your wedding isn't something *to get through*. It's supposed to be about what you want. What you both want?"

Mike chuckled. "Wait a minute. You mean I'm a part of this? That's news."

Allie rolled her eyes. "Mike. Please. I need you on my side. This is hard enough as it is."

Mike, Eleanor thought, was the prototype of a Nebraskan farmer. Medium height, stocky, strong build. He wore a beard that he didn't always maintain—much to Marilyn's dismay—so it was hard to know if he was handsome or not.

Allie thought he was, though. Allie thought Mike was the single best man in the universe.

Eleanor knew because Allie looked at him like Eleanor used to look at Max.

"Allie, I'm on your side," Mike told her. "Always. And I'm trying to do everything you're asking. But Eleanor's not wrong. This should be about us and what we want. You know what we didn't want? This party. You know what I don't want? Having to go out with every male relative you have as part of my bachelor party. Your uncle's been hinting at strippers all night. I'm not looking at naked women with your creepy Uncle Bob."

"Uncle Bob is not creepy," Allie whispered.

Eleanor nodded and mouthed, *Sooo creepy.*

"Guys, I know you're trying to help. But you're not. You," Allie said, pointing at Eleanor, "don't know what Mom has been like."

"I don't know my own mother?"

"You don't know what she's been like about this wedding. Everything has to be different than last time. Everything you didn't do, I have to do, and it all has to be perfect. She's scheduled no less than five dress fittings. Seriously? How many times do I have to see if a dress fits?"

Eleanor tried to swallow her irritation. She felt the guilt, but it was unreasonable. She didn't want her sister to suffer because of her elopement, but at the same time this was her mother's doing, not hers.

"Why did you agree to it? You are a grown woman, about to get married. Why can't you say no to her?"

"Because I'm the only one who cares about making her happy," Allie fired back. "And she knows it. Why can't you ever say yes to something?"

"I'm here, aren't I?"

"Yes and already complaining."

"Time out," Mike intervened. "This is getting heated, and people are starting to notice. We all promised to play nice."

Eleanor checked herself. Mike was right. This party, which was stressing her sister out already, wasn't the place to challenge her to say no to their mother. And, she had to admit to herself, maybe she wasn't as unaffected as she thought she could be.

It's not like any of this would bring back particular memories.

There had been no engagement party. No bachelor party. No large ceremony. No family and friends.

Just her and Max in front of a judge in a small town in Nevada. He'd given her a bouquet of daisies to hold.

Eleanor lifted her head, looking around the room for Daniel. She saw that he was talking to her cousin, Marissa.

Check that. Her cousin Marissa was desperately flirting with him. He seemed unaffected. A point in his favor as Marissa was quite attractive.

Then Eleanor turned to focus on her sister again. "You're right. I'm sorry. If you're willing to be whatever you need to be for Mom, then I'm willing to be whatever you need. I want this to be a happy time for you."

Allie nodded. "Okay, well, get ready. Here she comes, and she doesn't look happy…like at all. She must have run out of something. Please let it not be the liquor."

Eleanor saw her mother approaching, and it was true. She was nearly ashen. Her makeup unable to hide whatever had shocked her.

"Eleanor," she began, then stopped. She put her hand over her heart and took a few breaths.

"Mom, what is it? Are you having chest pains? Do we need to call an ambulance?"

Fear gripped Eleanor. A sudden heart attack was how they had lost her father all those years ago.

"No, it's nothing like that. Just a shock. We have a…guest. I've asked him to wait in your father's study. I don't want to upset the party and ruin Allie's night. Eleanor, come with me. Just you. Alone."

Eleanor had no concept of why her mother needed her alone. Or why a guest had to be sent to her father's study. An old high school friend? Or more likely a frenemy. There was Tony Santino, whom she dated for a while in high school until he ended up cheating on her with her best friend. Definitely not someone she would enjoy seeing again. Then again, there was no reason why he'd be here tonight. He'd been three years ahead of Allie in school.

Marilyn turned the corner, then stopped in front of the door to the study. Really? Whoever was inside was so startling he needed to be shut in?

"Mom, what is this?"

Marilyn was wringing her hands, clearly upset.

"There's nothing to do," she said eventually. "You'll just have to go in. I'll go let your sister know what's happening."

With that, her mother left. Cautiously, Eleanor opened the door. Inside was a man. He stood by the windows. Tall, his back to her. His hair was dark with a little gray woven through it. Something about the way he held himself. His hands clasped behind his back. His legs separated like the floor was the bow of ship and he needed the extra balance.

She knew that pose. She knew those shoulders. But of course, none of that was possible.

Then he turned. His face was weathered, more weathered than three years ago. But it was his face.

The face of her dead husband.

"Hey, Nor."

Immediately she bent over and threw up the champagne she'd been drinking onto her pretty Jimmy Choo pumps. It was as if her whole body was rejecting what she was seeing.

He took a step toward her, and she held up a hand to keep him at bay.

"How is this happening?" she muttered, still bent over.

"I know this is a shock. I didn't know how else to do this. I came home and my parents—"

"Your parents are dead. You're dead."

These were two things she knew to be true. A year after Max was officially declared dead, Harry and Sarah were in a car accident. As Max had been their only son, Eleanor, even though she'd been trying to get a divorce at the time of their son's death, was their only remaining family. She'd been listed as the emergency contact.

She'd arranged the funeral, the sale of their home. But she'd kept the cabin in the mountains. How could she not?

"I didn't know how to find you. I did some internet searches. I found your company, but then I saw the announcement of Allie getting married. It mentioned the engagement party tonight. I knew you would be here."

"Stop talking," Eleanor snapped. She couldn't process this. She couldn't accept the fact that she was seeing him again. He was dead.

For more than two years, he'd been dead.

For more than two years, she'd been dead.

"You died," she said as if she had to explain some fundamental truth to him.

"I didn't."

"How?"

He sighed. "That's a very long story."

She looked at him. Full-on. It was only then that she realized she had been looking at him like he was the sun. Indirectly. As if she would go blind if she stared at him full-on.

"You're here," she said. "You. Are. Here."

He nodded. "I am."

The door opened.

"Eleanor, are you all right? I saw you come in here alone. Oh, hello. And you are?" Daniel said, looking over at the stranger in the room.

Eleanor finally was able to stand straight. Her stomach no longer in jeopardy of upheaving anything. Her knees were shaky, but she was fairly certain she wasn't going to faint.

"Daniel, this is…this is…"

"Max Harper," Max said, reaching out to shake Daniel's hand.

Daniel's eyes got wide. "Oh, my goodness. You're…you're…"

"I'm Eleanor's not-dead husband."

CHAPTER THREE

"AND YOU ARE?" Max asked.

He knew. In his heart of hearts, he knew coming back here now might be too late. But he had to try. Of course she would have moved on. Of course she would have remarried.

She might have done that even if he hadn't been declared dead.

He looked at her again because he could. Because he was alive, standing in her family home—a place he'd been to on a couple occasions during their short marriage. He knew she was experiencing shock. But it wasn't all that different for him, either.

Because there was a time when he never thought he would see her again.

Eleanor.

She'd always been beautiful. Long, chestnut hair, dark brown eyes. Lips that were a smidge bigger than they should, which made every man around her want to kiss them.

Two and half years had only added to that beauty. Instead of the young woman he'd first met, full of all the hope and excitement of the future that was coming, now she was fully a woman.

He'd loved that young woman. Desperately. This person he wanted to get to know. If she would give him a chance. If this man wasn't who Max suspected he was.

He held his breath waiting for the introduction.

Waiting to hear the word *husband*.

"I'm Daniel Reynolds. Eleanor's date for this evening. And this suddenly got very awkward."

Date. Not husband. Not boyfriend. *Date*. The relief was palpable.

Max turned his attention to Eleanor, who was slipping out of her shoes.

"I need to run upstairs and freshen up. Max..." It was as if she was having a hard time saying his name, like she could barely push the word out of her mouth. "Max...you need to stay in here. I don't want to needlessly... upset anyone."

Except the door swung open, and Max turned his attention to the newest arrival.

"It's true! Oh, my God. You're alive. Max!" Allie ran to him and flew into his arms. He caught Eleanor's sister and swirled her around.

"Allie," he said into her pretty, soft brown hair. Finally. Someone who was actually happy to see him. Happy that he was alive. He'd adored Allie as if she'd been his real little sister. He'd known the feeling was mutual. Now, here she was in his arms, clinging to him.

Quite the opposite of her sister, Eleanor.

After too long a moment, he finally set her down. "Look at you. You're all grown up."

She beamed at him, and he wanted to ingest that smile because it was something else he never thought he would see again.

"This is— I can't even… How is this possible?"

"Apparently, it's a very long story," Eleanor said.

A man walked in behind Allie, then shut the door.

"Mike," Allie said, clearly getting emotional. "It's Max. He's alive."

"Better than dead, I imagine," Mike said, obviously trying to keep things light.

Max liked him instantly.

"A lot better than dead," Max agreed.

"Mike Davies."

"Max Harper."

Max shook the man's hand and assessed him. A little taller than Allie. A little stockier. He had a firm handshake and made direct eye contact. And when he looked at Allie it was as if the only thing that mattered right now was how she was dealing with the situation.

Yes. Max approved of Mike. As her pseudo older brother, he knew that would mean something to Allie.

"I don't know about anyone else, but I need a drink." This came from Daniel. The Date. "Can I get anyone anything?"

"Bourbon," Max said. "If you have it."

"Of course we have bourbon," Eleanor said as if he'd suggested something ridiculous.

She was flustered. She was still processing. She wore a stunning navy dress, and suddenly he realized he wanted everyone to leave so that he could be alone with his wife.

"Okay, okay," she muttered. As if she was a general coming up with a game plan. "Here is what we're going to do. Daniel, if you would be so kind to bring the bottle of bourbon back here, that would be great. I'm going to clean champagne off my favorite pair of shoes. Allie and Mike, you have to go out there and mingle. If you stay in here, people will wonder what's happening. I don't want anyone to see him."

"Why not?" her sister asked. "He's alive. It's not like he has to be hidden."

"Allie," Eleanor snapped again. "Please. I get you're happy to see him. But I think we all need to remember…how things were between Max and me…before…"

"I died. Except I didn't."

Eleanor looked at him then, and he remembered that expression. It was her way of telling him to go shut it. He'd missed that look. He'd missed everything about her.

Daniel. Date. Not boyfriend. Not husband. *Date.*

He could work with that.

"Eleanor…" Allie said as if this was something she was willing to put up a fight over.

"Allie, do what your sister says," Max said. "This isn't going to be easy. For any of us. We'll catch up later. You can tell me if this guy is worthy of you."

She beamed again, only this time it clearly wasn't for him. "He is. He so is."

Mike took Allie's hand and led her out of the room. Daniel left behind them. Then it was just Eleanor and Max.

"You could have called," she accused him.

"I didn't have your number."

It wasn't a lie, but it wasn't the full truth, either. He'd looked her up online. He knew she was the founder and CEO of a start-up company called Head to Toe. That had been his original plan. To find the address of her company. To see her there.

But when the engagement announcement popped up under his Allie Gaffney alert, this had seemed like a better opportunity. More personal.

They were also the only family he had left.

Max thought he would be coming home to two devastated parents and a ticked-off almost ex-wife. He hadn't expected his parents' deaths. How could he?

He'd been by the graveyard. He'd seen the headstones Eleanor had picked out for them. He knew that she'd made sure they were buried with all the respect and dignity they deserved.

She'd done that for them even though she'd left him and wanted a divorce.

"You could have found a way…to make this easier," she said. "This…it's too much."

"Nor—"

"Don't call me that," she snapped. "No one calls me that anymore."

"This was never going to be easy."

She nodded, at least acknowledging that.

"I need to…" She paused as if she had lost her train of thought.

"Change your shoes," he offered. "They look pretty expensive."

She lifted her chin. "I have a company."

"I know you do. I told you, I looked you up. It's how I found out about tonight."

Warily, as if he was some kind of predator, she backed away from him. "You need to stay in here."

"I'm not going anywhere."

Then she hesitated again. "Are you hungry? We have lots of food."

"Yes. I'm starving actually. Anything sounds good."

Again she nodded, then not turning her back on him—he liked to think because she liked seeing him standing in front of her—she left the room.

Max took a seat and blew out a breath. He figured the hardest part was over.

Then, almost instantly, he knew that was wrong.

Getting his wife back. That was going to be the hardest part.

MAX WAS ALIVE. Max was alive.

Eleanor thought if she said it a thousand times, it might penetrate her reality. But alternately she had to remind herself that, in some corner of her brain, she never really thought he was dead.

He had never felt dead to her.

But that was silly and based on feelings, not on facts. His ship went missing, lost at sea. Max had been declared dead. She'd grieved. Then she'd grieved again when Harry and Sarah died.

She'd stayed close with them despite the situation between Max and her because, at that point, there had been no reason to hold on to grudges. It hadn't mattered that Max had picked his job over his wife, because Max was dead.

Now he was here. Alive. Saying to her in that very serious way he had that he wasn't going anywhere.

Because that was so like him.

Showing up two and a half years later at her sister's engagement party undead wasn't meant to be dramatic or shocking. It was simply the most expedient way he had of seeing her again. Eleanor knew that.

Max wasn't drama. He wasn't show. He'd always been substance.

It's why she had always believed in their love, which, while it had been happening, had been so overwhelming. Because Max wasn't the type of man to have passionate affairs. Which meant their passion was something else. Something different. Something built on a foundation.

Until the foundation wasn't strong enough to handle another research trip. At least not for her.

Eleanor needed five minutes to escape. She needed to change her shoes, brush her teeth to get the taste of stale champagne out of her mouth, and, mostly, she needed to think.

She made her way through the crowd of

guests hoping she was doing an adequate job of not looking like her life had just been up-ended.

She ran upstairs toward her bedroom with her mother trailing after her.

"How is this possible?" she asked quietly.

"I don't know."

"Well, didn't you think to ask him?"

"Mom, I'm a little stunned right now, so could you back off?"

"No, I will not back off. Forget the fact that he's pulled this rising-from-the-dead stunt. Don't forget how things ended between you two before all that death business. You were devastated when you came back from Norway. I don't want to see that happen again. Say the word, and I'll ask him to leave this house right now. Your cousin Robbie can toss him out if he refuses."

Robbie was the tallest of the cousins and wouldn't have been able to move Max an inch if Max didn't want to be moved.

"No."

That much Eleanor knew. First, he had to tell her what happened. She, at least, deserved that. Then...there was so much more to work out.

His parents' estate, which she'd held in a trust for the past year because she was not exactly sure what to do with it, was one thing. Not to mention the tiny little detail that he'd never actually signed the divorce papers. So, now that he was legally alive, she was still legally married to him.

"Please tell me you are not actually happy to see him again. That man broke your heart, if you recall."

No, he hadn't broken it. He'd shattered it. Stomped on it. Then threw it overboard for chum. Then he went and ruined all of that by dying so that, instead of hating him, she'd missed him with every ounce of her being.

"No. I mean, yes, I have to be happy he's not dead. But it's not…I mean, of course I'm over him."

They reached the top of the stairs, and her mother pulled on her arm. "Eleanor Jane Gaffney, look at me and tell me you will ever be *over* Max Harper."

"It's Eleanor Jane Gaffney Harper, Mom. Remember?"

"Actually sometimes it's easy to forget because I wasn't invited to the wedding, now, was I?"

It was almost comical. Here Marilyn was threatening to throw Max out of the house by force if necessary so that he couldn't emotionally hurt her daughter any further, but she was still making digs about how they'd chosen to get married in the first place. "Really, Mom? We're going to fight about the elopement tonight of all nights?"

Her mother let out a sigh. "No. We're not. I just need to make sure you can...handle being around him again. Daniel seems like a very nice man. I would hate to see you throw away any potential you have with him over *Max Harper*."

"Are you angry with Max because we chose to elope? Or because he left me? Or because he died, but now is actually alive?"

Marilyn seemed to consider that. "All of the above."

"Right."

"I told you it was too soon," Marilyn hissed. Reminding her daughter for the millionth time that she had advised Eleanor against getting married so quickly.

"Which is why we eloped," Eleanor said tightly. The argument, for all its repetition, never changed.

"Because you're impossibly stubborn."

Eleanor wanted to say she got that from her mother, but thought better of it. It would only lead down the same path this conversation always took them inevitably. Which was that Marilyn had been right and Eleanor had been wrong. Something her mother had reinforced when Eleanor had come back from Norway.

Because there was nothing a person wanted more while crying over a broken heart than to hear her mother's version of *I told you so*.

"I need to get down there and talk to him. But I need a few minutes to compose myself first. Please give me a little space, Mom."

"Just don't lct yourself get sucked in again. The last time it nearly killed you when it ended. Remember who he is. I told you then and I will tell you now, that man doesn't know how to stay in one place forever. So he may be alive and he may be back for now. But it's only temporary. Sure enough, there will be another assignment and another ship."

Eleanor hated to admit it, but her mother had a point. Max had nearly been her downfall. The thing she had almost not recovered from.

Until she did. Until she'd pulled herself out of the ashes of her failed marriage and built herself a company.

"Mom, I'm not going to get sucked in by Max. I remember how it ended better than anyone. Really. I'm fine. But we need to sort out the technicalities. Legally we're still married."

"Fine. I need to get back to my guests. You're sure you can handle this?"

"I've got it."

At least she hoped she had it. She was no longer a lovesick, twenty-six-year-old woman who was desperate to have her husband not leave her again.

Instead, she was a strong, independent woman who owned a successful business. A woman who was dating another man. A woman who had been hurt, but who had moved on with her life.

No. All she needed from Max Harper was a divorce.

First, though, she needed to feed him.

CHAPTER FOUR

MAX TURNED AT the sound of the knock. Instead of Eleanor, it was Daniel with the bottle of bourbon he'd managed to acquire. He held up the bottle, and Max nodded.

The man poured them each a few fingers, then handed Max his glass. Max took a deep sniff, letting it seep through his senses. Yet another thing he was getting to re-experience. Booze.

He took a sip and savored the heat of it melting down his throat.

"So you're Eleanor's…"

"Husband. Yes, I thought we established that. And you are her…date. How did you two meet?"

"I'm an investment banker. I look for opportunities with thriving young companies to take them to the next level. Eleanor has one of those companies. I pursued it…then I pursued her."

"Yes. I'm aware of the company. Head to

Toe. Fitting. She always did all my shopping. Said I had no sense for fashion, which I suppose I don't."

"She's got excellent taste. She picked this tie out for me. Do you like it?"

Max thought about that. It was a nice tie. "No."

Daniel tilted his head back and laughed. "I see. This isn't going to be a situation where you wish us all the best in our burgeoning relationship and fade out of the picture."

"I've been out of the picture for more than two years. Fading away is the last thing I want." He sure as hell didn't want his wife finding happiness with someone else. Not when he planned to fight for her.

"Look, man, you can't possibly be serious. You've been dead for over two years, gone for longer than that. Eleanor doesn't talk about you much, but she told me the basics. You were married for three years, gone for most of that time, on the verge of a divorce when your ship went missing. Any feelings you might have had, any she might have had, that's all in the past."

"You've known me for all of a minute and

offered me a drink, but you think you can tell me how I feel about my wife?"

"Your ex-wife," Daniel said pointedly.

"Technically, that's not true." Eleanor was back and shutting the door behind her. She had a plate piled high with food in her hands. She looked pale, but more in control of herself than she had been earlier.

Yes, she'd changed in two plus years. She'd grown into herself. And as much as he'd loved the woman she'd been when he married her, that was how much he wanted to know this version of her, as well.

"Daniel, I'm sorry. I know this is incredibly rude of me…"

"I don't know that there is etiquette regarding dealing with a husband back from the dead."

Max gave the guy some credit. He was smooth. Freshly shaven, expensive suit. He looked and acted like money. No doubt a fish out of water in Hartsville, Nebraska. Still, he'd come to the sticks for Eleanor, which showed she meant something to him.

Daniel was a man in pursuit of Max's wife.

It was something Max simply could not stand for.

"I need some time alone with Max. I don't want you to feel like I'm ignoring you..."

"But of course you need to ignore me right now. You and Max obviously have things to work out. I understand completely. If you don't mind, I think I'll head back to Denver tonight rather than stay at the B and B."

"So late?"

"It's only after nine, and with no traffic I should be home in three hours."

She nodded. "You'll text me to let me know you arrived home safely."

Daniel flashed a smile in Max's direction. "See how she cares about me?"

Max prevented himself from tackling the asshole, deciding violence wouldn't get him anywhere. Certainly not with Eleanor.

"I do," Max answered. "But wouldn't anyone, given they were asking you to leave in the first place?"

Another shut-it look from Nor. Max wanted to tilt his head back and shout to the world. For years he'd been lost, for weeks he'd been devastated by the knowledge of his parents' death. But now, finally, things were starting to make sense. Eleanor was telling him to shut his mouth with the power of a look.

He was here. With Nor. And regardless of Daniel and whatever it was they had between them, Max was still legally her husband. His plan was to hold on to that, if nothing else, with both hands.

Daniel flashed another smile, then very deliberately kissed Eleanor on the cheek. "Good night, my dear. You'll pass on my regrets to your mother and tell her I hope to see her at the wedding?"

"Of course."

Douchebag, Max thought. But he supposed he had to feel some sympathy for the guy. If the situation were reversed, he would also fight like hell to keep a woman like Eleanor.

Daniel left, and Max waited until the door was closed.

"He'll see her at the wedding? Didn't they just get engaged? And the wedding's not for a while? Pretty ballsy move if you ask me."

"Yes, well…I don't want to talk about Daniel."

"That's unfortunate because I do want to talk about him. He says you two have a *bur-*

geoning relationship. Can you quantify what that means?"

Eleanor opened her mouth, then snapped it closed. "I don't think it's any of your business."

"None of my business? My wife is dating someone and that's none of my business?"

"Oh, please, Max. Let's not pretend here. I'm glad you are alive… I'm, well, the truth is, in a way I feel sort of redeemed because I never truly believed you were dead. I thought I would feel differently if you were dead…and I didn't…but then I had to accept it. So I did. But just because you are back doesn't mean anything has changed between us."

"You're right about that," he said.

She nodded. "Good. It's important that we are on the same page here."

"I agree. Can I eat?" He pointed to the plate of food.

"Sure. Sorry. I know you said you were hungry. You've obviously lost weight."

He smiled at that. "I've been back in the States for a few weeks, Nor. It's not like I haven't eaten since being rescued."

"I asked you not to call me that."

Max sat on the sofa. He set his drink down

and picked up the plate of food. Steak tenderloin, mashed potatoes, a corn cake—Marilyn's special recipe. And some broccoli, which Nor knew he wouldn't eat, but she put it on his plate because she thought it was important he eat more vegetables.

"Looks good. All my favorites. You remembered."

"Don't," she warned him. "Don't try to read anything into that. It's food."

Max held up his hands as if in surrender, then reached for the corn cake and took a bite. Savoring the flavors in this mouth.

"God, that's good. You can't know what it's like to eat nothing but fish for years."

Cautiously, like she was in the room with a caged beast, she sat in the chair across from him.

"I guess it's time you told me your long story."

ELEANOR ALMOST DIDN'T want to hear his story. It seemed like it would make her too invested in him again. It would be better to simply to tell him to leave now. They could handle everything—the divorce, his parents' affairs—all by mail, then that would be the end of their story.

Nothing so dramatic as a lost ship, a story of survival and returning from the dead.

But she supposed she had to know.

He shrugged after eating the last of her mother's famous corn cake, literally licking the crumbs off his fingers.

"We ran into a storm. Not sure why the captain didn't have more notice. But it was a bad one. Waves coming over the bow, we just took on too much water. The ship was going down. We took to the life rafts with not much hope. I broke my leg in the effort. The pain was... I don't like to think about it. We drifted for days. The two crewmen with me died. I thought I was going to, as well. I don't know if I passed out or slept. The next thing I knew, I was on a fishing boat and someone was giving me water. We landed on a small island off the coast of Iceland. Completely isolated from any kind of civilization. The best I can equate it to would be like an Amish community here in the States.

"A small village, not more than a few hundred people. Living off the land. Good people, but they spoke a Nordic language I didn't understand. They had absolutely no English. My femur was broken. Their version of a doctor set it, but I couldn't put any pressure on it for months. Then I was sick with pneumonia. I didn't think I was going to survive that either without antibiotics. I pulled through it eventually with their natural treatments. It was months before I could walk, months after that to get my strength back. Then it was just a matter of waiting for a commercial fishing boat to pass by, one with the ability to communicate to the people of the village and me to explain I needed to get on it somehow. There were months I thought I would be stuck there for the rest of my life. I fished with them. I ate with them. Then, finally, a commercial fishing boat appeared. I was able to talk to the captain, convince him I needed to leave. The crew sailed me out to the ship, and eventually I made my way to Iceland."

That was also typical Max, she thought. She'd counted no less than three near-death experiences, but he brushed over all of that like they were just facts in some other person's story. As if none of it touched him.

"And when you got back to Iceland?"

"It was difficult. I wasn't…used to people. It took me time to assimilate again. Eventually, I made my way to the U.S. consulate. Told them who I was and what happened. They reached out to the university to tell them I was alive. I kept trying to call my parents… It wasn't until I got to the States that I learned what happened. Someone from the university met me at the airport. Told me about the accident. Told me what you had done for them. Now here I am."

"Here you are," she whispered. "I'm sorry. For your loss of them. They were such good people. You should know that after you…after you were declared dead I spent time with them. The three of us were together. We all sort of overlooked the fact that I had been in the process of divorcing you."

"I didn't think you would do it," he said quietly. "I never thought you would really leave me."

"I know."

Max leaned forward, his hands loosely linked together. "I'm sorry I left, Nor. God I'm so sorry."

"Not sorry enough that you didn't turn around and get back on another ship."

She watched him wince. As if she'd slapped him. She hadn't meant to cause him pain. Or had she? When the four months passed, she'd been determined to resist every effort he would make to win her back. Positive in the knowledge that he would have taken the first plane he could to be by her side.

That he hadn't even bothered to try winning her back had been crushing in its own way.

"I had a plan," he said roughly.

"You always had a plan, Max. It just didn't include me."

"You're wrong."

Eleanor sighed. "It really doesn't matter. It's all in the past now. What's important is what we do moving forward."

"I agree." He nodded. Then he reached for the bourbon and took a healthy slug.

"So, I'll talk to my attorney when I get to Denver. I'm sure the papers are still on file somewhere. She should be able to just pull up the file. There was no property. I had saved some of your old books and things. I had given them to your parents after... But when I settled the estate, I donated anything I could to the local library. Sorry."

"Don't be. I was dead."

"And I gave all your clothes to Goodwill. Sorry again."

He laughed. "Again, don't be. I lost about twenty pounds, and I haven't been able to put it back on. I'll need new ones anyway."

Eleanor could see that. Max was tall at six-two, but two plus years ago he'd been broader in the chest and stomach. Now he looked leaner but still just as strong. Like a man who had been doing physical labor on a fishing boat for the past few months. Rather than just gathering data.

She didn't want to think about how he looked, though. The changes to his body underneath the clothes.

Yes, a naked Max should be the last thing on her mind.

Eleanor swallowed. "In addition to the divorce papers, I can have my attorney draft a letter that will transfer the trust fund I set up with the residuals from your parents' estate to you. Also I'll need to deed over the cabin to you."

That had his eyes perking up. "You kept the cabin?"

"I…I couldn't let it go."

He liked that. She could tell by the expression on his face. As though it was important to him that she couldn't let it go.

That cabin was where they had spent their honeymoon and handful of other times when they had just wanted to get away. The cabin was a place filled with memories of making love for hours on end. With no thought or care in the world but each other.

Mentally, Eleanor had to push those memories away, as well.

"I'm glad. I would have been sad to have lost that, too."

She couldn't be sorry, then, that she saved it. He'd lost more than two years of his life, and, in that time, he'd lost almost everything else. His parents, the house where he'd grown up, all of his things...her.

"It's getting late. Most folks will start to clear out soon. That couch you're sitting on pulls out. You can sleep here tonight."

"Not going to kick me out like you did Danny boy?"

"His name is Daniel, and I didn't kick him out. He had a room at the B and B in town. You know Mom's rules."

"No ring, no bed. Why do you think I needed to marry you so quickly?"

She tried to smile. She really did. But all she could feel right now was sadness. The shock of seeing him again was starting to wear off, and all the old feelings she'd had when she left him were still there.

"Good night, Max."

He stood and walked over to her. She noticed he had a slight limp. A broken femur in the middle of the frozen Norwegian Sea. On a life raft with two people who were already dead. She couldn't imagine what he'd suffered. Couldn't let herself think about how it made her feel to know that he was out there on the ocean alone.

"I think I've left you with a misconception. You said that just because I'm back doesn't change anything between us, and I agreed."

"Yes. So?"

"When I said nothing's changed between us, I meant it. I loved you when you left, and you loved me. As far as I'm concerned nothing has changed."

"Max…"

"Nor, I screwed up. I know that now and I've

had more than two hard years to think of what I had done. But I'm back now, and I'm never going to leave you again."

Eleanor shook her head. This was what she'd been afraid of when the four months had passed, and he came back from his expedition to find her gone. That he wouldn't simply accept that she had left him. That she wanted a divorce. That he would fight for her.

She remembered thinking she would need to be as strong as she had ever been in order to resist him. Because he was right. She had still loved him when she left him.

"I don't believe you."

"It's the truth. I'm never setting foot on a ship again."

"That's obviously a natural fear you have right now. But in time that will heal and you'll—"

He grasped her around her upper arms and gave her a small shake. "Nor, look at me. I'm not getting on a ship again because I'm afraid of the water. That's not the reason. I'm not getting on a ship again because I'm not leaving you. Ever. I cost us years of our life together. I know that. So, I'm not wasting another second of it. I was prepared, if I came back here to find you happily married with two kids and a dog, that I would have to accept it and let you go. But a couple dates with Danny boy? No way. I'm fighting."

"This is pointless, Max. It's been too long. Surely you don't think I can still be in love with you after all these years?"

He stared into her eyes, but, honestly, she had no idea what he would find there.

"Then I guess I'll have to make you fall in love with me all over again."

"That's not going to happen." She wouldn't let it happen. She would never survive a round two with Max Harper. She was sure of it.

"Then prove it. Come to the cabin with me. A couple days for me to spend some time with my parents' stuff. Grieve them with me. Please, Nor. At least give me that."

"It won't change anything between us."

"Then there should be no reason why you can't come," he said as if he'd beaten her in a contest of logic.

"Except that I have a company to run," she said, exasperated that he wouldn't even consider she had her own life. Wasn't that what he'd told her to do? Find something that was important to her. Have a passion for something that wasn't him.

"I know." He smiled. "Head to Toe. I told you I found it when I was looking for you. You're considered one of the fastest growing start-ups in Denver."

She would not be pleased he'd read that about her. She would not feel an ounce of pride.

"A couple days. You can bring a laptop to work remotely. We need, if nothing else, more closure to our relationship. That's all I'm asking."

If she was going to do this, then she needed to get something out of the deal.

"Fine. A couple days. You'll see there is nothing there between us anymore. No relationship to be salvaged. Then you'll agree to a non-contested divorce. Deal?"

He took a step back, and she almost took a step forward as if to follow. Such had always been her attraction to him. Just like a magnet.

He held his hand out. "I agree to divorce you if I can't make you fall in love with me again."

"Max..." she growled.

"Take it or leave it."

Everything inside her was screaming that this was a mistake. That, in fact, the only shelter from the Max Harper storm would be to find whatever island he'd lived on for the past two or so years and go there—where he would never find her.

Instead, she shook his hand.

"HOLY COW? CAN you actually believe this is happening?" Allie spit out the toothpaste she had in her mouth so what sounded like a question to her probably came out as a mumble to Mike. Then she made her way to her bedroom through the connecting door of the bathroom.

She should probably lower her voice. Eleanor's room, after all, was on the other side of the connecting bathroom door.

"That your mother is letting me spend the night in your room without the benefit of marriage vows?" Mike asked. "No, I can't believe this is happening."

Allie took a minute to check out her fiancé in her bed. He was right. This was a stunning development. They had dated for three years, had lived together for one, had been engaged now for a few weeks, but this was the first time Mike had ever even been upstairs in her room.

She'd given him the guided tour of her young-girl years, her teenage-crush years, her longing-to-go-to-college years…that had hurt. Showing him what she hadn't accomplished.

Two years of community school was all her mother had thought she needed. With an associate degree she could work at a bank, or as a receptionist in an office. After all, what on earth would Allie ever do with a four-year degree when she'd only ever been a B student in high school?

Unlike Eleanor who had gotten straight A's.

The awful part was that Allie hadn't known what she wanted to do. She couldn't say that she wanted to go to college for any particular degree. Couldn't fight for it like Eleanor had. Then again, Eleanor hadn't won any battles with her mother. Marilyn hadn't thought college was necessary for her oldest daughter, either.

Eleanor had just figured out a way to do it all herself.

Including getting married.

"I don't mean that," Allie said. "But it is

crazy. It was like after Max showed up she had no fight left. I told her you'd had another drink as a result and couldn't drive, and she was like... *Fine. But be respectful and for heaven's sake don't...do anything.*"

Mike laughed. "I am so going to *do* stuff to you when you get in this bed."

Allie giggled. It might be the biggest rule she'd ever broken. Wearing her tank top and pajama bottoms, she threw herself onto the bed and Mike's chest. He let out a hard woosh as if she crushed him, even though she knew she hadn't.

"What I meant before is isn't it crazy about Max?"

"Guy returns from the dead? Yeah, I'm pretty sure the last time I saw that happen it was on *General Hospital.*"

Allie bit her bottom lip. "This is going to wreck her, but I hope...I really hope she gives him a chance. For her own sake. They loved each other, you know?"

"Like us?"

Allie smiled. Yes, she knew she loved Mike as much Eleanor had loved Max. "It was different for them, though."

"Different how?"

"They had all these obstacles to overcome. Mom thought they hadn't dated long enough to get married. Then, of course, she opposed the elopement. Hence the Allie-and-Mike-wedding extravaganza. At every turn they faced something and then in the end…it was just too much to overcome."

Mike snorted.

Allie knew that snort. He wasn't buying her story.

"What?"

He shrugged. His big bear shoulders lifting out from her soft, daisy yellow duvet. "You told me the story, Allie. Max left her for his work. She left him because she couldn't do it anymore. That's not a love that sticks. That's a love that doesn't stick in hard times."

"But you don't know what would have happened if he hadn't been gone for more than two years. Two years, Mike! They could have worked things out. I know Max. He wouldn't have let Eleanor go without a fight."

Mike rolled onto his side taking her with him so that he half lay on top of her, his big, bearded, Midwest-farmer face so precious to her, there for her to touch and stroke.

"I'm never going to leave you. No matter what."

Allie smiled at him. "Me, either. I'm not trying to say our love is any less than theirs. Circumstances were just different for them."

"Tell you what. You want an obstacle we have to overcome…tell your mother I don't want a bachelor party with your creepy uncle, and I want to cut the guest list in half to make this thing more about us and the people we love. Let's see if we can fight through that, because I know that's what you want, too."

Allie cringed. "I know she's difficult…"

Mike shook his head. "It's not about her being difficult. That's Marilyn Gaffney and I accept that. This is about what Eleanor said to you tonight. What do you want, Allie? And what are you willing to fight for, for us? Eleanor was willing to fight for Max. She got him, then she left him. Maybe he wins her back, maybe he doesn't, but I know this. No matter what happens with Max, it won't be your mother's call. It will be Eleanor's."

"You're saying I'm a pushover," Allie muttered, feeling herself get defensive.

"I'm saying I want you to start fighting for yourself and what you want. Because the next thing you know, I might be that person you're just trying to make happy all the time. If that happens, you'll start to resent me, and that will stink up a marriage like cow shit in a barn."

"You have such a way with sayings."

"I'm serious, Allie."

She knew it was a fault. Knew it was something she had to find within herself. But tonight was her engagement party, and it was over, thank God! Mike was in her bed and Max was not dead.

Which meant, in some ways, Eleanor might come back to life, too. The way she had once been.

"Fine. You want me to speak my mind?"

"I do."

"Well, this fiancée wants an orgasm, and you're going to have to be pretty crafty about it because my mother cannot hear a thing."

Mike smiled. "I can give that a shot."

Allie smiled as he slid under the covers, and, after a time and an amazing orgasm, she knew Mike had, indeed, given it his best shot.

CHAPTER FIVE

"ARE YOU INSANE?"

"Mom…" Eleanor groaned.

"I think it's a good idea," Allie chimed in.

They were sitting together at the breakfast table. Last night Marilyn had made sure Max had pillows and a blanket. She'd also made it clear she thought it best he leave early in the morning before any of the staying guests woke and found him in the house.

Too many questions and all that.

Eleanor had given him her number so he could reach her, and, true to his word, he was gone before anyone woke up.

The house now empty of guests, it was just Eleanor with her mother and her sister as she explained over eggs and bacon where Max had been for the last two or so years, everything that had happened to him, as well as how they'd left things between them.

It was strange, Eleanor thought. How different she felt waking up this morning. For one, her first thought hadn't been about Head to Toe and what her schedule looked like for the day. For another, it was the crazy realization that Max was once more alive.

Not just in the physical sense. But alive for her. A decision she needed to make. An action she needed to do. It was like breathing for the first time after holding her breath for so long.

Maybe for more than two years.

"It is absolutely not a good idea. Do not encourage your sister," her mother said to Allie.

"Mom, it's the most expedient way to end this," Eleanor said.

Because that was what she told herself. A few days with Max. Closure on their relationship. A real end to what had been the most significant relationship of her life.

"I know Max. He's stubborn as heck. He'll beat this drum endlessly until he realizes the truth. That what we had is over. Then he'll give me the divorce, and I can finally move on with my life."

Her mother rolled her eyes. "Right, because in the two plus years since his *death*, you've been able to move on. What was Daniel? Maybe the third person you've been out with in two years."

"Technically the fourth." Three blind dates—one of whom canceled at the last minute, but she had agreed to the date so that counted—and Daniel. Then there was that other incident, the one she didn't like to think about because of how it made her feel. Certainly no reason to inform her mother of that.

"I was married for three years, Mom. It's not the strangest thing that, while I was growing my business and getting over my failed marriage, then the death of my husband, dating would not exactly be a priority for me."

It was another argument she'd had often enough with her mother in the past two and a half years. Marilyn wanted her to move on, find another husband and start having babies.

Eleanor hadn't been ready for any of that.

"Tell yourself that if you want, but I know you. And him, although not as well. Whatever it is about him, it acts like some kind of drug for you. You let him charm you for a few days, and you'll find yourself falling back under his spell. Telling yourself, he's changed. Then eventually when he goes away again, you'll find yourself where you were when you decided to leave him the first time. Do you really want to go through that again?"

"Of course not," Eleanor mumbled. It wasn't possible she could fall for Max again. Having him and losing him had hurt too much. It left a wound that, if she was being honest with herself, hadn't ever healed.

Allie was shaking her head.

"What?" Eleanor asked her.

"Eleanor, it's simple. I know you were devastated when you left him. The reason you were was because you did love him. And when he was reported dead, you were like a zombie. I know because I lived with you for three months after. That's how worried we were about you."

"Right. That's why it can never happen again."

"You say that like you can control it. Do you still have feelings for him or not? If you do, then you owe it to both of you to hear each other out. You guys…just being around you guys as a teenager, I could feel the love. It's what made me certain that it was real and it was out there. It's why I was certain when I fell for Mike. I know it's been a few years. I know this is like something out of a bad soap opera. But you're both to blame in this."

Eleanor's jaw dropped. "How can you say that? He left me!"

"And you left him. When you knew he loved you more than anything. When you loved him more than anything. You gave up on the two of you first, and that's not like you."

"Allie!"

"You did, Eleanor," her sister insisted. "And now I can say, being in a relationship myself, that ultimatums never work. They just piss everyone off."

"I can't believe you're taking his side."

"I'm not taking anyone's side. I'm telling you to think about how you felt when you saw him last night…"

"Sick. I felt sick when I saw him last night and ruined a perfectly good pair of shoes," Eleanor informed her sister. She felt the same queasy feeling now looking down at her plate of eggs with the yellow yolk running everywhere.

Because Max loved eggs. It was their Sunday morning tradition.

Shit.

She hated that she now seemed to be in this perpetual spiral of memories, good and bad, of her time with Max.

"What about Daniel?" her mother insisted.

"What about him?" Eleanor asked.

"If you do this thing, if you spend this time with your ex-husband, can't you see that you'll ruin any chance you have with him?"

"Mom, Daniel and I have been on a few dates. Our second one ended with me telling him he needed to leave because my long-lost husband, aka Indiana Jones, just returned from out of nowhere. I don't think there is much of a future there for us."

"Hmph," her mother sighed. "A nice man, a man of means, a handsome man who wants to date you. That's who you can't see a future with. But Indiana Jones, that's who you are pining over."

"I'm not pining," Eleanor insisted.

"You haven't answered my question," Allie told her. "Do you have feelings for him? Mom obviously thinks you do."

"Of course I do. It was right there on her face when she saw him again. Like she couldn't look away."

Was it? Eleanor wondered. Was it right there on her face?

"Mom, I don't get it," Allie said. "If you think she still has feelings for him, why wouldn't you be encouraging her to see where those feelings might lead? He is her husband, after all."

"Because he's going to hurt her," Marilyn told her younger sister. As if Eleanor wasn't sitting at the same table. "Again. And frankly, I don't want to have to pick up the pieces. If you were supportive of your sister, you wouldn't want that to happen, either. You're getting married in a few months. Right now, everything is hearts and flowers with you. All you want to see are happy endings and that's simply not reality."

"Just because you and Dad weren't happy, that doesn't mean nobody can be happy," Allie said.

Which caused her mother to gasp.

Eleanor, too, for that matter. Allie was the quiet one. The pleaser in the family. It was Eleanor who was usually the source of her mother's upset.

"Allison Ann," her mother said tightly. "How could you?"

Immediately, Allie ducked her head. "I'm sorry, Mom, but it's true. If Dad hadn't died so young, can you honestly say you wouldn't have thought about getting a divorce?"

"Never. Divorce was simply not an option for us. Your father's and my relationship was... complicated. We'll leave it at that."

"All I'm saying is that Max and Eleanor are complicated, too. Maybe she shouldn't write off her marriage so easily."

Starting to get annoyed with the way they were talking about her, Eleanor said, "I love how my little sister is telling me how to live my life."

Allie picked up her orange juice and flashed Eleanor a bright smile. "Only when I'm right."

Marilyn picked up her plate and silverware, signaling an end to both breakfast and this conversation. She would, however, have the last word. As always.

"Eleanor, you're going to do what you want. You always do. But know this—men don't change. It's simply not in their nature. He left you, and he will leave you again. Trust me on this."

With that, she took her plate to the sink, then left the kitchen in typical dramatic form.

Eleanor looked at her sister. "What were you thinking bringing up Dad like that?"

"I'm tired of lying about it. We know how it was like between them right before he died. But of course, we can never discuss it. I guess maybe what you said last night at the party rubbed off on me. It's time to start speaking my mind. Time to stop worrying about everyone else's feelings. I think you should give Max a shot. More than that, I think you're looking for any excuse to do it."

Eleanor sighed. "He hurt me, Allie. Bad."

"You were different then. Not as independent as you are now. I don't believe what Mom said at all. I think people do change all the time. Things happen. Max almost died! You don't think that had any effect on him figuring out what he wanted in his life going forward?"

"Another good point. What if wanting me back has nothing to do with me?" Eleanor suggested. "What if this is just him clinging to any part of his former life? He came home to nothing."

"And if it's not?"

How did she explain her fear? "I wasn't enough for him back then, Allie. As much as he loved me, I wasn't enough."

"I don't believe that for a second. Because if that were true, really true, he'd divorce you and move on. You know what I think? Maybe back then you weren't strong enough to handle what you two had. Maybe that's why those long trips freaked you out. I know for a fact that's not the case now. The Eleanor Harper I know can definitely handle it."

Eleanor eyed her sister. "When did you become so wise?"

"While you all weren't looking. Look, you already agreed to go away with him. I'm just saying keep an open mind."

Eleanor didn't know if she could agree to that. But she also knew the only way out of her marriage was through Max. Nothing was going to change that. And this was the last piece of his parents that he had. Being there for him wasn't out of the question.

"I should probably tell Daniel."

"Yeah, if it were me, and I had no shot with you, I would want to know, too."

"Allie!"

"Sorry. I'm Team Max hashtag teammax. All the way."

It was Sunday night, and Eleanor was in her condo in downtown Denver. She'd spent the past few hours dealing with emails that had backed up over the weekend. Now that she was caught up, there was no use denying to herself that she'd been putting off the inevitable.

Eleanor looked at the phone in her hand. It would be so easy to just text Daniel. Did one dinner and one disastrous engagement party really make him eligible to be updated about her personal life?

That justification was a defense mechanism, though, and she knew it. She'd found him attractive. She'd had a nice time on their date. Who knew? Maybe a few more dates and she would have slept with him.

Eleanor thought about what that would have meant. If Max hadn't come back when he had. She would have been still married—

Then she remembered the man she had never told her mother about. The *incident*. That one aberration when she'd been traveling to California to meet with another woman who had a similar company, although geared toward women. Rather than be competitive with one another, the other owner had encouraged Eleanor and had given her some amazing advice.

That night, alone at the hotel bar, she'd been approached by a handsome man. Another business traveler. He'd offered to buy her a drink and she'd—

Eleanor couldn't think about that. It had been so awful. So...off the entire time she'd been with him. The morning after had been worse. It was as if she'd betrayed Max in some fundamental way.

Now she knew that she had. It wasn't fair she should feel so guilty about it. She thought he was dead at the time. Never coming back.

You're going to have to tell him.

Eleanor shook off that thought, as well. She had absolutely no obligation to tell Max anything. He should have been her ex-husband by the time that encounter happened. She would have been free to do whatever she wanted with whomever she wanted.

Not that she had since. Much to her mother's despair, Eleanor had had absolutely no interest in getting serious with anyone until Daniel had pursued her. Even the few blind dates she'd accepted, mostly suggestions from Selena, she'd argued against until ultimately she capitulated.

But with Daniel pursuing her hard and talking about things as if they could be long-term between them, Eleanor realized if she was going to marry again, have children, dating was going to be a requirement.

The truth was after that first date, she'd been interested in seeing him again. Yes, he had a tendency to come on a little strong, but still, she'd asked him to Allie's party. That had to mean something.

Which meant he was owed an explanation for why she was going on an overnight trip with her husband.

Taking a deep breath, she brought up his contact information on her cell and punched the button to call.

"Eleanor."

See, she thought. No silly nickname. Just her name. Like everyone else called her.

"Daniel, how are you?"

"Better now that I'm talking to you. How did things work out?"

"Uh, as good as could be expected."

"So he's agreeing to the divorce. That's excellent news."

Eleanor winced. "Not exactly. He's got some conditions."

"Conditions?"

"You know that cabin in Breckenridge I told you about? That was actually his parents' cabin."

"Interesting fact, but somewhat off topic."

"Not really. He wants me to go there with him for a few days. To help him grieve his parents. To talk things out. Bring some closure to our relationship. I think—I think…it's something we probably need to do."

"I agree," Daniel said.

Eleanor blinked. It wasn't exactly the reaction she was expecting.

"Oh. Good. I thought…well, I wanted you to know."

"I'm glad you did. It means you respect that there was a brief connection between us."

"Was?" Eleanor repeated, interpreting his use of the past tense as his way of telling her it was over between them. She thought about how she felt. Maybe a little sad, but relieved, as well. With Daniel came all this pressure. For things she wasn't ready for with him.

"Or is, I suppose. Depending on how those few days go."

Eleanor frowned at the phone. "I'm not sure I understand what you mean."

"Eleanor, in a classic twist of irony, I was trying to explain to you at the party that dating you was not easy because there was always the ghost of Max Harper to overcome. Then said ghost walked through the front door. Not exactly what I was expecting. But the reality of him, while more real now, doesn't change anything. You need to decide where you are with him. Because until you do, you'll never be able to really move on with your life. I want to date you, Eleanor. I want a relationship with you. I've made that clear. But I don't want any of that if, deep down, you're still hung up on your would-have-been, could-have-been ex-husband."

"I am over him," Eleanor insisted. She had to be. She couldn't possibly believe that, after more than two years of thinking he was dead, all the feelings she'd had for him were still there.

Could she?

"Take the time with him. Find out for certain. And remember, it took me three attempts just to get you to agree to dinner. Three times. And I'm very rich and very handsome."

Eleanor chuckled.

"I did mean what I said, Eleanor. I care about you, and I want what's best for you. If that's me, then I would feel honored. But I think you need to consider how thick and heavy those walls you've built around yourself are. More importantly, you need to figure out why you put them up in the first place. Those answers, unfortunately, are with Max. If you can't, I don't know that you'll find that happiness I'm hoping for you."

"You should also add very insightful to your list of qualities," Eleanor said.

"Did I mention I'm also very well endowed?"

Again Eleanor laughed.

"You're laughing. No man likes laughing after a statement like that."

"You're being nice to me. Thank you."

"Because I'm a nice person, Eleanor. Mostly. Good luck. With everything."

"Good night, Daniel."

"Goodbye, Eleanor."

Eleanor disconnected the call and thought about what he said. Could she admit she had walls? Yes, absolutely. She'd loved. Harder and deeper than she'd imagined she could. She'd given Max everything for a time. And for a time, he'd given her everything in return.

Then he'd broken her heart, and she never wanted to feel that pain again. So, yes, she was cautious with men. Wary of them. She had made Daniel jump through hoops before she agreed to go out with him.

But if she had walls around herself protecting her from other men, then she imagined she would need walls, a moat, barbed wire and any other fortification she could make to keep her safe from Max Harper.

CHAPTER SIX

MAX LOOKED UP at the brick building and checked his phone to see if thc GPS had taken him to the correct spot. They were going to drive up to the cabin together, but Nor had told him to pick her up at work. It was after seven in the evening, which he thought was fairly late, but he'd already made the mental note not to comment.

The first thing they needed to do was get rid of the baggage between them. With a hatchet if necessary. Then there were truths about what they had been, and the hope of what they could be still.

It was going to require total honesty. It was going to mean bringing up a lot of pain for both them.

Max knew, without question, their time together at the cabin was going to be way harder than surviving a shipping accident for more than two years.

He reached for his right thigh and rubbed it in a gesture that had become almost instinctive. The pain was there as a low, dull throb. But at this point, he felt it was manageable and saw no need to cling to drugs he'd been given when he had his physician check out the break to make sure it had been set properly.

The doctor offered him the option of surgically breaking it again to reset it a little straighter, but at the end of the day, with a break in a bone as large as a femur, that pain was going to linger.

So no drugs, no surgery, just a barely noticeable limp and some low, dull pain. It was something he could live with. Max walked toward the building until he found his way up to the fourth floor. A label on the elevator told him it was the headquarters for Head to Toe.

Nor, I can't be the only thing in your life. That is not the woman I married. You're not this clingy, weak thing. You're Eleanor Gaffney. You're the girl who shook off her small town, who found a way to put herself through school. You were going to rule the world. What happened to that girl?

He remembered every word of that fight. Every moment, ever tear.

He'd been cruel. Looking back on it, it had been easy to see that he'd been dealing with his own guilt. Guilt for leaving her when he said he wouldn't again so soon after being back. Guilt for bringing her to Norway where she had no support at all. Not from family or friends. Not from him when he was away.

But the work…back then it had always seemed so important. So imminent. As if he didn't take this one trip, didn't find this one bit of data, then all would be lost for everyone. Because he'd had to show everyone the ocean was changing. Not just that sea levels were rising but that the chemical components of the seawater were experiencing a negative impact by the increased planetary temperature.

It was yet another thing living alone in a solitary community, separated from the outside world for two years, had taught him. He'd been truly arrogant about his work.

The truth was he wasn't that important to the world. The world got along just fine without him. Other oceanographers took his place, continued his work and published papers related to ocean changes and climate warming, and nobody missed a beat.

The elevator dinged, and the doors slid open. He was greeted by a massive, open space loft. Certain areas seemed to be defined by opaque separators. It was quiet, though. There was no one behind the front desk, even though the phone was still ringing. He assumed there was some automated system set up to answer the phone.

It was the other eerie thing about being back in the States after so long. The noise. Even on the outskirts of northern Norway it had always been quiet, peaceful.

Boring if there was nothing there for a person to do.

Nor had never complained. Never about the quality of her life there. Only ever about him leaving her alone.

He made his way through what he felt was a natural corridor to the rear of the office space. That was separated by a halved glass wall. Two equally sized offices on either side.

The one office was empty.

The other office was occupied by two women huddled over a laptop, their backs to him.

He had a moment of thinking that it wasn't a very protected space. That the elevators weren't locked and how anybody could just walk in and steal from them. Or something worse.

Then he realized for all he knew there was security. Maybe she'd left the elevator open because she knew he was coming. And for all he knew the offices in front of him could have locks. The glass could be bullet resistant.

Max recognized the long, wavy, dark hair of his wife. Even from behind, even after all this time, she was familiar to him. The shape of her. The way she cocked her hip and tilted her head.

The woman next to her had short, blond hair, wore a neat white suit with pants that tapered to thin ankles that were supported by ridiculously high heels.

He tapped on the glass of what he assumed was the door. The two women jumped, then turned.

Nor bit her lip, clearly not sure if she was happy, nervous or dreading seeing him again.

The other woman looked to Nor and said something.

He could read Nor's lips. *Yes, that's him.*

It wasn't a given that the glass was bullet-proof, but it was obviously soundproof.

Eleanor stepped forward and opened the door. "Hi."

"Hi," he answered, feeling suddenly foolish. As if he was back in high school showing up for his first date.

"Max, this is Selena. She's my number two at Head to Toe."

The woman stepped forward with her hand outstretched. There was hesitancy there, but Max could see she was trying to give him the benefit of the doubt. He took her hand.

"Nice to finally meet you, Max."

He nodded, because he wasn't sure what to say to that.

"You both look busy. I can come back later if you need to continue working."

Nor shook her head. "I think we're done."

"We're done. After all, once you've spent all your money there is not much to do after that." Selena chuckled.

Nor tucked her hair behind her ear. A gesture he knew meant she was shy about something. "I have my stuff in the trunk of my car.

I have an SUV. I thought for the trip it might be better. I wasn't sure what you were driving…"

"A rental. Probably best we take your car."

"Okay. Why don't you bring your car inside the garage? You can park, and we'll move your things to my car."

"I was hoping you could…" Max shrugged, not sure what he wanted. Maybe to be in on the joke Selena thought was so funny. Something about spending all their money. "Show me around the place. I would like to see…everything you built."

Eleanor extended her hand to the space outside her office. Max saw lots and lots of open desks and phones and computers. "That's pretty much it."

"It's not it," Selena interjected. She nudged her hip into Nor's. "Go show him. He should see it. What you've done."

Eleanor took a deep breath and let it out. "Okay. Come on."

She led him out the door of her office, and he fell in line like a helpless puppy who could do nothing else but follow where his master led. He tried to remember if that was the way she had walked before, or if the three-inch heels she was wearing had changed that. He liked the way the shoes made her legs look. That was for certain.

Then he had to stop thinking about her legs and focus on what she was saying.

The customer service department was responsible for answering questions, taking orders, signing up new customers. Dealing with returns and unhappy clients. A tough job, but she required that her people be upbeat and "on" all day.

The words were spilling out of her lips, and he was desperate to soak in each and every one. He wanted her to know he was paying attention. He wanted her to know that her life and everything that had happened to her in the past few years mattered.

It was just hard to concentrate when even the sound of her voice was its own kind of delicious turn-on. The way it made him feel. Like he could listen to her and only her forever.

I think I love you, Max. Isn't that crazy?

He remembered the first time she'd said it. They had been in bed together, the morning after they first made love, just days after their first date. Too soon, he thought and yet not soon enough. That's how greedy he'd been for the words.

I love you, Max. More than anything.

She'd said that to him on their wedding day. Standing in front of a judge, knowing she was going to be on the receiving end of her mother's wrath and her younger sister's disappointment. Except he'd been so sure of them. Absolutely positive they had been doing the right thing at the right time.

I love you, Max Harper.

It had been the last thing she'd said to him. The words he'd lived on for over two years. Believing that after everything he had done, no matter what had happened in those years, that those words would always be true.

"Our IT staff is pretty robust, as well. Obviously, as an online business, our access to the internet and our customers' access to us is incredibly important. One day of lost sales can have a major impact on our revenue for the month…"

He nodded. Because it was important that he hear the words. Important that he understand her life, her business, what was important to her. Except it was hard to hear over the sound of the voice that had once told him she loved him.

She stopped when they made it back to her office. A basically square room with the different departments broken apart. "And that's really it. Shipping is two blocks away in another building. That's where we warehouse our products and handle boxing. I also subcontract with a delivery service that handles pickup and delivery."

"It's amazing. You're amazing."

She smiled, but he thought it wasn't totally genuine. As if she didn't quite believe him.

It wasn't that Nor was a stranger to him. She could never be that. Not when he knew what each quirk of her lips meant, how every gesture showcased all her different emotions. No, she could never be a stranger to him.

But she was trying to be.

A distant stranger, an old acquaintance. Not the woman who used to tell him how much she loved him. Not his wife. She was putting up roadblocks between them. Signs that all said, Don't Get Too Close.

He had a few days to change that.

Suddenly, he feared it wouldn't be enough.

"Shall we go?"

Max nodded. "Is Selena okay here by herself?"

The other woman had returned to her own office and seemed to be furiously typing on her computer.

Nor looked at him then as if she was reminded of something about him. Max thought that was a good thing. The more she remembered about him, the more she might remember she liked him.

Of course, that was a two-sided coin. The more she remembered what drove them apart, the more help she'd have to secure those walls she'd put up against him.

"She's fine. The building is security monitored, as is the garage. We both work a lot of late hours. I wasn't sparing any expense on our safety."

"Smart."

"A single woman has to be."

They both flinched.

Then she shrugged in apology. As if she hadn't meant to say it so harshly.

"I'll go get my car. I parked on the street."

She nodded tightly. "Meet me in parking area D. It's toward the back."

They separated, and Max made his way to his car. He started it, then drove toward the building where she must have done something to open the garage door automatically. It was easy enough to follow the letter coded system to the rear of the garage, and as she pulled out in her white BMW SUV, he slid in to the spot next to hers.

He got out of his car and popped the trunk. He grabbed his new duffel, the one he'd had to buy after losing his well-worn, well-traveled one to the Arctic Ocean. It still felt stiff over his shoulder.

Nor had gotten out of the car and popped the trunk for him. As he tossed in his bag, he noticed she was wearing pants but had removed her suit jacket. She still had on heels, and he wondered if she wanted to change. It was only an hour-and-forty-or-so-minute drive to where they were going in the mountains, but still...

Then he realized she was heading around to the passenger side of the car.

Of course, she thought he would drive. When

they were together, he always drove. It was his thing. He preferred to be in control behind the wheel.

Then he considered the discomfort in his leg. Driving hurt like a bitch. Even the short, fifteen-minute trip to get to her building from his hotel had been enough to set it throbbing. Most of the trip would be along the highway, but he knew once they got into the mountains, it would be a lot of slowing down around steep curves.

He didn't want to spend his time thinking about his damn leg. Not when there was so much they had to talk about. He needed to be focused, but he also didn't want to seem weak in her eyes.

She stopped as she reached for the car door. The sound of her clicking heels coming to an abrupt halt.

"You've changed your mind," she said softly. "You don't think this is a good idea."

"No!" *Shit, shit!* The fact that she asked the question meant she was having doubts. He didn't want her to have any doubts, but it's not like he could expect anything less.

"No," he said a little more calmly. "I want

this. I want us to have a chance to talk. More than anything. I just…my leg. It's my right, so driving puts a lot of pressure on it."

"Oh. I didn't realize."

"How could you?"

She ducked her head; then as if it were the most casual thing in the world, she circled back to the driver seat and hopped inside.

"All good," she said. "Let's go."

Let's go. Right, he thought. As if this was no big deal.

It was probably the first time ever in their relationship when he'd admitted to any kind of weakness.

Because he'd thought men shouldn't be weak. Men should be strong and in control and leading, always. Which was crazy, too, because his dad had not been that kind of man at all. He'd been kind and good, so humble.

It had had more to do with Max spending so much of his post-college years at sea with salty shipmates, and even saltier captains. As the *research nerd*, he found out pretty quickly he had to hold his own on a ship with hard-core, hard-nosed seamen, or his ass would have been kicked to the shore fairly quickly.

There was no time or space for weakness at sea. Something several men of Max's acquaintance died knowing.

Still, worrying about not being able to handle the drive would make him look like a stupid, macho man.

Even if he was a stupid, macho man.

Max made his way to the passenger door, then got in. He felt a wave of embarrassment creep over him, but then he quickly got over it. This wasn't about being the cocky sonofabitch he'd once been. The man who thought he could leave this woman over and over again without any repercussions.

This was about him turning the page and being not the man *he* thought he needed to be. But the man Nor needed him to be instead.

That man had a bad leg. And an almost two-hour drive into the mountains wasn't something he was physically able to do without a lot of pain. He wondered how she would process that.

"Weird, huh?" he finally said.

She nodded. But she smiled a little. "It's probably something you never knew about me."

"What?" he asked. He hated the idea that there was anything he hadn't known about her.

"Well, the truth is I really love to drive. It's like one of my more favorite things. And this baby handles curves in the road like a man's hand on a woman."

Max barked out a laugh. "Why did you never tell me?"

She gave him a look that said he should know better.

"Right. I probably would have insisted. Still...something I didn't know about Nor Harper. I like it."

She smiled again, and he thought maybe she liked that, too.

CHAPTER SEVEN

"SO WHAT DID Selena mean about spending all your money?"

The road stretched out before them. It was dark, but Eleanor had no problem navigating the familiar roads out of the city until they had finally reached the highway. She was still reeling a little from the fact that she was the one driving.

It made sense, of course. His leg hurt, so she should be the one driving. But deep down she knew it was so much more than that. Max had acknowledged a weakness in front of her.

Eleanor tried to think back to their years together. Had he ever done that?

She didn't think so.

"Nor?" he asked again, reminding her that there had been a question.

"Oh. That. We decided to move ahead with our plans for expansion. It's a pretty big risk, and we took out a significant loan. Now we have to hope it pays off. For the foreseeable future, however, financially speaking, we're a little vulnerable. It's the first time it's been like this. So far, it's all been about organic growth. This is the first time we're taking matters into our own hands. It's scary and thrilling and—" She glanced over at him. "And I'm boring you to tears?"

"No, not at all. I'm fascinated. I want to know every minute of your life that's happened in the past few years. I don't want you to skip any of it."

She wasn't surprised by his sincerity. It made sense for a man who had been disconnected from his life, now permanently disconnected from his family, to want to find comfort in something familiar. Someone familiar.

"Max, I know you think this trip is about some kind of reunion. I even understand why. You must be terribly unmoored."

"Unmoored," he repeated thoughtfully.

"But you have to understand we can't go back to what we were. It's not possible."

"I don't want to go back. I was a selfish ass then. I want to go forward. So let's do this another way. I don't want to know everything that's happened to you in the past few years so I can catch up. I want to know everything that's happened to you, so that I can get to know Eleanor Harper. A woman I would like to get to know."

Eleanor didn't say anything. She knew she had to be careful with Max. He was charming at the worst of times. So easily able to get past her defenses when she wasn't on guard.

Because you love him.

No! Loved *him. Past tense.*

"There isn't much in my life beyond the company."

"How did you get started?"

"I came back home after…well, after. We had subleased our apartment, so my only option was to stay with Mom in Nebraska."

Max barked out a laugh. "Once again necessity is the mother of invention. You were desperate to get out of the house, so you were forced to come up with a brilliant business idea."

Eleanor chuckled. "Something like that. There are only so many times you can hear *I told you so* before your choices whittle down to murder or escape. I didn't want to go to jail for murdering my mother, so..."

"Head to Toe was born."

"I liked to shop for you. I always did. You hated it, and you were awful at it. Anytime I said you needed a new shirt or pants you were sure to come home with something dreadful. And I know it didn't matter to you, but as your wife...it mattered to me how you looked. I thought of all the men out there in the world who don't have someone to tell them what matches nicely, what doesn't. What's new in clothing trends, what's out. I happened to be in the mall, and I guess I was feeling sad, knowing I would never shop for you again. I found myself in the men's section looking at ties, and this poor young man walked up to me desperate for help. He had an important job interview, and could I help him put together a decent outfit. He must have thought I worked for the store, but I didn't hesitate. I took in his hair, his coloring and sent him out of the store in a guaranteed job-winning suit, shirt and tie."

"Did you ever find out if he got the job?"

Eleanor shook her head. "It didn't matter. I just knew it was something I could do. I was a business major. I had the basic concept of what I wanted to do. The rest was a matter of rolling up my sleeves and getting down to work."

"And Selena?"

"She was my first hire. She's got great instincts when it comes both to clothes and business."

"You called her your number two," Max pointed out. "Does that mean she's a partner?"

Eleanor shook her head. "No. It's all mine. She works for a salary. I think if we grow, though, she'll eventually want a piece for herself. I'm considering letting her opt in, but only for a third of the company."

"You always did like to be in control," Max said, resting his head against the car seat even as he tried to stretch. She saw in her periphery vision he was rubbing his right leg again.

"Except with you," Eleanor said quietly. "Never with you."

Reason 1,952 why she shouldn't spend one second allowing herself to even consider giving Max a second chance. Their dynamic had been too lopsided for her. For him, too, she eventually came to learn.

He'd always been the one in charge. She'd

tolerated it because she'd loved him so damn much. That as much as he could make her crazy, he also made her happy.

It couldn't be the same now. As the owner of her own business, she knew instinctively she'd be less likely to put herself second to his every wish.

She couldn't imagine he would deal well with that. Then again, she couldn't fathom a scenario in which he would let her drive him, either.

"It would be different, Nor," he said as if reading her mind. His face was turned toward her, but she kept her eyes on the road. She found that the less time she spent actually looking into his face and his eyes, remembering everything that they had shared, was healthier for her.

"You say that..."

"I know it. You don't spend over two years in what amounts to solitary confinement not looking at your life and studying it. The mistakes you made. The paths you took that steered you off course. I know where I went wrong, and I know what I have to do to fix it. All I'm asking for is a chance."

Eleanor shook her head. "It's impossible. We should focus on the reality of our situation and moving forward."

"A divorce," Max said harshly.

"It only makes sense." She said it, and she knew it did make sense, but the word still grated. "Did you ever sign the papers I sent to you?"

"No," he said dully. "I tossed them in the trash."

At the time she'd wanted to make sure she had started the process so he would know how serious she was. So that when he came running after her, as she'd been so convinced he would, she would be prepared. Then, of course, he'd been dead, and there had been no need to do anything else to try to finalize the divorce.

Legally, she was single again.

Only now, he wasn't dead and she wasn't single. She looked over at him again, and she was struck by his profile. A profile she'd memorized every line and dip of. She'd memorized the sound of him breathing, the flicker of him blinking.

He was alive.

Her heart started to pound in her chest, and

she took a few deep—and quiet, she hoped—breaths to steady herself.

After a time he asked, "What kind of divorced couple would we be?"

It took her a second to process the question. "Uh, a divorced one."

"No, I meant what would we be like. The kind who go their separate ways and never see each other again? Or the amicable kind who still like each other and get together for dinner or brunch once or twice a month?"

Eleanor considered that. She couldn't imagine never seeing Max Harper again. She'd done that. For more than two years. Now that there was an option, she didn't want to do that again.

Still, dinner with him. Brunch with him. Casually sharing their lives.

"I would never move on," she blurted out unintentionally.

"Neither would I."

"So we're agreed. Us trying for some type of friendship...would be a bad thing."

"Nope. We don't agree on that at all."

IT WASN'T TOO LATE, just after nine, when they reached the cabin. It was outside of the snow slopes of Breckenridge. Far enough away that there was little to no tourist traffic. Close enough that, in season, it was easy to get a day pass to go skiing.

The long, winding driveway—or more accurately, dirt road—hadn't changed in years.

It was mid-September, and the air was just starting to change, but the snow was still a few months off. This was one of Eleanor's favorite times of the year to be here at the cabin. She wasn't the biggest skier, having grown up in the flat plains of Nebraska. The idea of sliding down steep slopes at ridiculously high speeds didn't appeal.

Max had said it was because she was a control freak.

She liked to call it sanity.

But long hikes through the Rockies, in the quiet woods where the most that could be heard were animal noises and running streams. That had been right up her alley.

She pulled up to the sleepy cabin situated on stilts to both get a better view of the front and back decks and to ensure safety from any critters large or small that might try to get in, since the stairs served as the single point of entry.

She turned off the engine, but she didn't move to get out right away. It had been years since they had been here together. It had been on their last break in the States, before returning to Norway and right before the Great Fight, as she had come to think of it.

She felt the occasion deserved a moment of silence. For their marriage, for his parents. For him, for that matter.

After his parents died, after she had buried them and sold the house, she came to this cabin by herself to mourn. Them, Max...her.

Because it had felt like that. With all the strange potential of her future in front of her, she had felt the need to grieve this lost side of herself. The side of her that loved, deeply.

She could hear Max's even deep breathing. She noticed he didn't move, either. She wouldn't until he was ready.

"Okay," he finally said after a few minutes. "I'm ready."

Nodding, she got out of the car. She popped the trunk and reached for the two bags she'd brought. An oversize tote that had everything she needed for a few days and a bag of groceries that would feed them for the same length of time.

He'd pulled out his duffel, and, together, they made their way in silence to the cabin. A two-person funeral procession. They climbed the steps to the second-level deck, and Eleanor fiddled with the keys in her hand until she found the one she was looking for.

She pushed open the door and the smell of pine and long-dead hearth fires greeted her. It never failed to please her.

It also was reminiscent of their tiny little home in Norway. Always cold, always damp, always with a fire burning but so clean and fresh-smelling at the same time. Like coal and oil had never made it that far north to contaminate anyone's senses.

They weren't so primitive to live without electricity altogether. A private generator powered lights and the television for occasional movie watching. Eleanor hit the light switch and instantly the cabin glowed to life.

She could feel him behind her. Could feel his tension. She wasn't really certain how to soothe it away. Technically, it wasn't her job anymore.

In fact, she told herself she shouldn't really

care how he was feeling. Other than general sadness for his loss. But that would be a lie. And maybe it wasn't so wrong for her to empathize with his grief. She had to stop thinking as if having any feelings for Max automatically meant she would be vulnerable to falling in love with him again.

They had been married. There were going to be feelings.

It was just about not letting them get out of control. That was what mattered.

"Nothing has changed," he said.

"No," she whispered.

Moving forward, she made her way to the kitchen. It was basically one large open room. The kitchen had a breakfast bar that looked out onto the dining room where, as a family, they used to gather to eat after a long day of hiking or skiing. Or in her case, reading and sipping hot chocolate in the ski lodge while the others skied.

The living room was sprawling, filled with big, brown, well-used furniture. The hearth was the feature of the room. A larger-than-average fireplace which took a lot of wood to fuel but provided heat for the entire space, including the two bedrooms that were on either side of a short hallway.

The flat-screen TV, the only thing that hinted of modernism in the old-fashioned cabin, was tucked away in a corner of the room. Sarah had declared it should be used only in case of emergency.

The cabin was supposed to be a place of family. Of talking and sharing. Of fighting. Politics, taxes, climate change. Of discourse. Of ideas. Max had come by his career in academics naturally as both Harry and Sarah had been academics. Harry in economics and Sarah in anthropology.

Together, they had birthed an oceanographic scientist.

All the way from Colorado.

It had been so far removed from her own home growing up. Even when her father was alive, the overriding theme of the Gaffney household was to never say the thing that shouldn't be said.

The thing that would upset everything.

Allie had dipped her toe in that water the other day over breakfast. Admitting that their parents, in the last years of their marriage before Dad had died, hadn't been happy.

It had felt like someone pouring a bucket of ice water over Eleanor's head. A definite shock to the system.

Not here though. Not in this space. There was nothing that wasn't said here.

"Just like it used to be," she muttered as she set down her bags.

Three and a half years ago

HIS PARENTS HAD left that afternoon. They hadn't said anything directly—Harry and Sarah would never be so gauche—but they looked desperately like a couple who wanted to leave their son and his wife to the business of making them grandchildren.

Something Max and Eleanor were more than happy to keep on practicing until they got it just right.

Naked, tangled up in blankets along the couch, Eleanor rested her chin on Max's chest and thought about the future that lay ahead.

"Let's stay here, Max. Let's not go back to Norway."

"Nor," he groaned even as he kissed her on

top of her head. "You do this every time. You're like a kid on a vacation who doesn't want to go back to school. You can't avoid reality forever."

Except there was no school for her waiting in Norway. There wasn't even work. There was tending house, trying to learn the Norwegian language and, mostly, waiting around for Max to get home.

"I'm not talking about staying at the cabin. Although, don't get me wrong, I could happily live in this cabin naked forever."

"Naked?"

She thought that might get his attention.

"Buck naked."

"Won't that get cold in the winter?"

"Not if I have someone around to keep me warm."

He growled again. "I'm the only one allowed to keep you warm when you're naked."

She lifted herself then, higher on his chest. The blanket fell, and his eyes dropped to her breasts which were now on full display.

"Focus, Max."

He didn't lift his eyes, merely raised a single eyebrow. His left. Always his left. "I am."

She reached out and lifted his chin so that

he had to look at her eyes. "I'm serious, Max. I'm not talking about staying in the cabin. I'm talking about staying in Denver. About settling down. Something more permanent. More stable."

"We talked about this, Nor."

It was an old refrain. When they had gotten married, he'd laid out his plans. His timelines. What he needed to accomplish out there in the world before he could settle into a life in academia, which was a lot of teaching and writing articles and books.

When she'd married him, the thought of the two of them traveling the globe, collecting data and potentially saving the world with his climate-change research, had seemed like the most glamorous adventure she could imagine.

The reality was months stuck in places far away from civilization with only Max and some fishermen's wives with whom she could barely converse as her only company. When the loneliness had started to creep in, Eleanor had told herself she was selfish and spoiled. What Max was doing, he was doing for the planet Earth. Something way more important than her.

But the time alone was starting to take its toll.

She didn't bother to counter his argument. There was nothing to counter it with. He'd told her what the plan was. She'd agreed to the plan. It wasn't like she had a leg to stand on. She just knew something was changing between them. The weeks apart weren't making the time when they were together better. They were making it harder.

Max always assumed they were like a rubber band. No matter how far they stretched apart, they would always snap back together into the exact same shape.

Eleanor, too, had once believed that. That no force could ever separate them indefinitely because what they had was unlike anything she had ever imagined. Certainly far more powerful than her own parents' relationship.

But now she was coming to see that the rubber band, when you continued to stretch it and stretch it and stretch it, lost some of that elasticity.

"I'm worried, Max," she said into his chest even as she ran her fingers across his hardening nipples.

"I'm not, Nor. We're a unit. And nothing is

going to change that. Certainly not a couple more months in Norway."

"You sound so certain."

"Because I am. Because I love you and you love me and nothing is going to change that."

"And babies?" She was still in her twenties. It wasn't as if they didn't have time. However, it wasn't something they could put off forever.

"And babies will come. Eventually."

She sighed.

"Trust me, Nor."

"Do I have a choice?"

"Hey," he said, and she could hear the concern in his voice. He jostled her enough so that she had to lift her head and look at him again. "Do you trust me?"

She nodded. Of course she trusted him.

"I'm not going to do anything I think might seriously hurt us. I know that much about myself."

"You love your work," she had to point out.

"I love you more," he insisted. "This isn't a choice between you and the work. This is about you and me doing what we can now while we can make the most difference. Putting it all out there for a couple years to make the most impact. That's what we agreed to do."

"But it's not *us* doing the work. It's *you*. I'm just the cheerleader on the sidelines."

"You ever go to a successful football team and *not* see a cheerleader on the sidelines? There is a reason for that. It's because what I do, everything I do, is for you, Nor. For you, our future, our children. You and I are a team. And don't think for one second any of the work I do would mean anything if I didn't know that I had you to come home to."

She smiled, or at least tried to. "Do you know now if you're going out to sea?"

He shook his head. "The funding is still up in the air. No one knows if it's going to go through or not. I can't see a trip happening for some time. Just a lot of shoreline research."

She lay against his chest, content to let him stroke her back. Long, slow slides of his fingers all the way up to her shoulders and down over her ass. Soothing but also arousing when, on every third down stroke, he cupped her cheek in his hand and gave it a squeeze.

"We're going to be okay," he said even as he began to intensify the strokes. "Because no matter what happens, we'll always have this. Us."

He proved his intent, by dipping his fingers between her thighs, feeling her desire, then pulling her up enough so that he could slide his now hard again dick up high inside her. Connecting them.

She gasped.

He hummed.

Yes, she thought. They would always have this.

CHAPTER EIGHT

"Nor. Nor?"

She was staring at the cold empty fireplace, and Max had no idea what she was thinking. Or remembering. There had been so many memories it was hard to sift through them all. He shut the door behind him and dropped his duffel.

Then he watched as she sort of drifted off into a trance.

Coming up behind her, he laid a hand on her shoulder. She startled.

"Sorry," he said. "You looked a little lost."

"I guess I was. This place…you know."

Yeah, he thought. He knew. Just standing here was hard. It was like he could see and hear his parents. The boy he'd been growing up. The reluctant teenager who thought this place was boring. The man who had started to see its beauty as he got older.

The twenty-six-year-old girl he'd brought here after their elopement.

The sex had been unlike anything he'd ever experienced before. It had never been deeper or more profound.

It had never been more freeing.

There was no longer any show to put on, no agenda to perform. Nobody to impress. Just two people who would spend the rest of their lives touching and sucking and kissing and coming.

Some people thought sex after marriage was boring or indifferent. He had always thought of it as the best sex of his life.

He closed his eyes and tried not to imagine how long it had been since he'd kissed her. Since he'd held her. Since he'd touched her skin and felt her desire.

The truth was he wasn't sure if he was really worthy of any of those things anymore. He supposed they would find out in the next few days.

"I'll start a fire," he said. It gave him a purpose, which he liked.

He took his time getting down on one knee to open the grate. There would be wood to collect from outside, the fire starter kit to assess in terms of how stocked it was. Many things to do. It would help him to focus on the present. Neither the past nor the future.

"I can help," she said, approaching to hover over him. He looked up, and he could see she was staring at his right leg, which he had spread out straight. All his weight resting on his left knee.

"Nor."

She turned to him, her face a picture in concern.

"Remember how back in Denver I let you drive me…"

She seemed hesitant as if it was a trick question.

"Yes."

"Let me build this fire."

Her lips tweaked. "You're such a freaking guy."

"Thank you. Thank you for that compliment. Now please allow me to retain my 'guy' self and make fire."

"You think that will help, don't you? That I'll be impressed even though it's simply a few logs, some kindling and a match."

"You always made the fire building sound so ridiculously easy. Building a fire is an art."

"Okay, Harry."

It rolled off her tongue perfectly naturally. It's what she always said whenever he quoted his father. Which Max liked to think he did a lot because his father was a very wise man.

But they both knew it wasn't really funny anymore.

"I'm sorry."

"I'm not ready to… I can't yet. You know?"

She nodded, moving toward the kitchen.

"Yep. I'll go unpack the groceries. I bought us some lasagna for tonight. All we have to do is warm it. That and some garlic bread I just have to pop into the oven for a few minutes. Thought it might be easier."

The number of things he missed about Eleanor, ranked in order:

Her face.

Her kindness.

Her courage.

Her lips, breasts, legs and ass. They were all tied.

Her ability to hear him, however, when he hadn't said anything at all. That might be number one.

It had been maybe the most defining thing

about their relationship. Even in the beginning. He didn't have to explain himself as he so often did when his thoughts got ahead of his words. It was like she existed as his own personal mind reader. Always knowing what he was trying to say. Always understanding what he was feeling at any given moment.

Could he say he'd been that for her?

Absolutely not. Because on that day when she was trying to tell him, so desperately, how she felt about him leaving, he'd never really *heard* her.

Reason 155 he'd been the asshole in their relationship. Which was why he needed to fix it.

That would come later. Right now, he had a fire to build. After he procured the necessary supplies, executed the logical procedures and finally lit the match, in seconds flames started to lick and dance among the logs.

Behold, he thought. *I have made fire. Surely if I can do that, I can get my wife back.*

A few minutes later, he was still staring at his accomplishment, wondering how one went back to the beginning and fixed everything he'd done wrong, while at the same time, clinging to what had worked between them.

Soon, she was next to him again. Two glasses of red wine in her hands.

Of course, he thought, because they were having lasagna for dinner, and red would pair with that better than white.

A moment like this and he might tease her about her mother. How in so many ways she was like Marilyn. Even if it was unconsciously.

He reached to take the glass she held out. Then she went to sit in the leather recliner. By herself. He got up, slowly and trying not to groan too loudly, then sat on the couch.

It felt awkward being out of their normal positions. He'd always sat on the couch, but she'd always sat on the couch with him. Curled up along his side. Never once had he thought it was annoying or invasive. To always have her pressed against him whenever he sat on a piece of furniture had been the natural order of things between them.

He had no doubt her decision to take the recliner was deliberate.

Sipping on his wine, he noted the quality and sighed.

"It's like everything is new again," he said.

"I can imagine that must be what returning from the dead feels like."

He turned to her. "I felt dead. I knew I wasn't. If nothing else, the constant pain was a reminder of that. But I was gone from the world I knew. You, Mom and Dad, my fellow researchers. Everyone was gone. And as kind as…well, frankly, giving as the villagers I stayed with were, it wasn't the same. Even after two years they were still strangers to me."

"That's not like you," she noted as she sipped on her wine. "You were more likely to make friends wherever you went. Any time we went out to a bar, you always left knowing and liking more people than before you went inside."

"I know. It was definitely a departure. I couldn't blame it on just the language, either. I had found my way along in plenty of other places where I didn't know the language. It could have been the trauma of the wreck itself. I needed to heal from that along with everything else that went wrong with me."

Max dropped his head along the cushions of the couch. He'd felt this way before. As if the stuff he'd had inside his head was too heavy to hold up with his neck alone. Besides, it was easier not to have to look at her when he said the bad stuff.

"I tossed the bodies off the raft, Nor. I knew when I did it there would be no proper burial. No cremation. An empty casket at best for their families to bury. I knew that, and I still did it anyway. Because they were dead and I wasn't and it seemed...I don't know. Wrong to hold on to their bodies. As if it was the only way to stay alive. Like if I had kept them on the raft, then they would pull me down with them."

"Max," she whispered.

He shook his head. Trying to push the thoughts away. The macabre wasn't exactly romantic.

A timer dinged, and the distraction was a welcome one. He set his wine on the table in front of him and pushed himself to standing. "I'll help."

She nodded.

He'd been good at that, he thought. Trying to remember every moment of their marriage. What he'd done well, where he'd failed. Helping with household chores had been a no-brainer. Mostly because his mom had insisted he know how to take care of a house. From cooking, cleaning and doing the laundry. To landscaping, home repairs and plumbing.

Max had never shied away from any of it, having his parents as role models. They had been partners. Until the end. Max supposed there was some solace in the idea that they died together. He couldn't imagine one living after the other had passed. A true fifty-fifty couple.

He couldn't say he and Eleanor were like that. Mostly because Eleanor had always been more geared toward doing everything herself. Something else she'd picked up from her mother. From necessity after her father died. But Max wondered if Marilyn's role had been that of caretaker to both children and home prior to her husband's death.

"Do you miss your father, Nor?"

Max was in the kitchen, ready to make himself useful, but he could see there was no point. The lasagna was out of the oven and steaming. She was cutting up the garlic bread. Before she would have gone so far as to make a salad, but obviously, she'd worked right up until they left.

She served the meal as she considered his question.

"The easy answer is of course I do. Every

day. And in some ways that's true, but the reality is he's been gone for so many years that there are days when I don't think of him. When I realize that, it always makes me a little sad."

"You think in fifteen years I won't think about Harry and Sarah?"

Eleanor set his plate in front of him, then touched his arm. It was a simple gesture, her hand resting on his forearm. But it reminded him how much more he wanted. There had been a moment, driving up to the house in Nebraska, when he'd thought about what kind of welcome he might receive. He didn't know if there was going to be a husband and children. He didn't know how much anger was still going to be between them.

So he'd had this fantasy. Where he walked through the door and she ran to him. Where he pulled her into his arms and held her with every ounce of the strength he'd recovered. Where he pulled her down with him to the floor and ravished her and she relished in it.

That obviously didn't happen.

For now, he would take the touch of her hand on his arm.

"You're never going to forget them. That

I can promise you. And there will always be something you do or something you say when you'll realize it was because of them that you're doing it or saying it. Sometimes I sigh…"

"Who, you?" He was teasing her. Nor sighed. A lot. It was her way of thinking before she spoke.

"Yes, me," she retorted. "I know I do it, but it wasn't until after he was gone that I realized how much I sounded like him when I did. It was his sigh. His habit that I picked up. So even on those days I might not think about him, or miss him, all anyone has to do is ask me a question, and I let out a sigh…and he's with me."

"You're being nice to me."

"Well, you were dead. Seems like the right thing to do."

He huffed. "Smells good."

"I can't take credit. I've become a huge fan of all those hardworking chefs behind the scenes at the grocery store who take pleasure in feeding me."

He found the cutlery drawer and got knives and forks for both of them. They sat at the kitchen bar rather than at the larger dining table and dug in.

"So Allie is getting married." It seemed like a safe topic to bring up. More geared to the future rather than their past. A place, he thought, to start to talk to one another again.

"She is. I'm thrilled for her. Mike is an amazing guy. I know this because he's willing to go along with all of Marilyn's plans for the wedding."

"I imagine she's happy they are not eloping." It wasn't lost on Max that his first big mistake in dealing with Marilyn Gaffney was depriving her of a wedding for her daughter. For the most part, it had been downhill from there.

He was going to have to change that, he thought. He had just taken it for granted that his mother-in-law wasn't his biggest fan. Like one of those clichéd married-man jokes that he and his mother-in-law never got along. Now Max could see how wasting family, even family through marriage, was not an option for him.

"Oh, I don't know if they even had a choice. Which, of course, upsets me. For Allie. The next coming months should be about what she wants, what Mike wants. I'm afraid none of that is likely. It's going to be about what Marilyn wants, and I don't know that Allie is… I don't want to say strong enough to fight her. It's more like she's resolved herself to not fighting her."

"She was always the peacemaker," Max noted.

"What do you mean?"

He took a sip of wine and looked at Eleanor, feeling that rush of euphoria that he was looking at her again. Relearning all her expressions. The expression she wore now, he knew well. Always those lifted eyebrows, like he'd surprised her with something when he knew he hadn't.

"Nor, puleeze."

"What?"

"Allie has spent, what I imagine has been every day since your father died, desperately trying to make you and your mother get along. You could see it. She would tie herself up in knots trying to please you both. It makes sense. She was only what…eleven when your dad died. The earth had to shake under her feet when that happened. Making sure her mother and her sister continued to be a family unit would have been paramount in her mind."

"You know I always used to hate it when you did that."

"What?" He didn't want to do anything Nor hated.

"When you were smarter about my family than I was. I feel guilty. It was Allie's engagement party and…"

"And your dead husband crashed it and ruined it. I'm sorry about that."

Eleanor smiled. "Yes, while that had been very dramatic, it's not what I feel guilty about. I was already giving Allie grief about not standing up to Mom. I was pretty sure she didn't want the engagement party to begin with, but capitulated to the will of Marilyn Gaffney. Maybe she did, but I shouldn't make her feel less for that. I would have apologized…"

"But you had other things on your mind."

Another tweak of her lips. "Just a few."

"Am I going to have to beat up that guy you were with? Don't get me wrong, I'll try, but there is a good bet I might lose. I'm only at about maybe eighty percent of my former strength."

"Daniel knows where I am this weekend. Not that I owed him any explanation, but I felt it…it was the right thing to do. He thinks it's a good thing. To get some…closure. He thinks I wouldn't be able to move on without it."

Carefully, Max set his glass down and looked at Nor. "I don't really want that."

She sighed. "Max…"

"No," he interrupted. "Hear me out. You came here with me for your reasons. I asked you to come with me for mine. But you need to know, I may be only eighty percent of my former self, but I'm going to fight, Nor. I'm going to fight like hell. Dinner was delicious. Thank you. But truth be told, the company was better."

That said, Max picked up both their empty dishes and washed them in the sink. When everything was cleaned and put away, he filled their glasses with more wine, and together they made their way toward the fire.

Again, she chose to sit alone.

Again, Max said nothing.

Together they just sat and sipped their wine and looked at the crackling flames. And Max thought it was enough.

For now, she was here, with him, for whatever reasons she had.

Yes, it was enough.

For now.

CHAPTER NINE

I'M GOING TO fight like hell.

Eleanor stared at the wood beams above her head and thought about what that meant. There was nothing left to fight for. She didn't understand how he couldn't see it. Even before he'd been proclaimed dead, before they had suffered more than two years of separation—something that few couples might reasonably find their way back from—their marriage had already been over.

She'd left him.

No, he'd left her. She had to remember that. She needed to feel the anger that had pushed her out of her marriage. It would sustain her as she reconciled herself to the fact that Max Harper was alive again and in the world she lived.

The knock on her door wasn't soft or gentle. It was done with intent for her to hear it.

"Max?"

He opened the door, and the silhouette of him against the moonlight that filtered through the windows of the cabin struck her. As if everything that had happened since the party had been a dream. That he wasn't really alive, but a ghost from her past she had to deal with before she could move on with her life.

Then he stepped into her bedroom, their bedroom, and he was, all of a sudden, very real.

"Is something wrong?"

He didn't say anything for a moment, and she could see he was wearing sweatpants and a T-shirt. Nothing familiar to her. Nothing old and worn as had been his custom. Of course there was nothing like that around for him anymore. Everything he'd ever had was gone.

She also noticed he had a pillow under his arm, a blanket slung over his shoulder. Like a little boy who'd had a bad dream in the night and was looking for someone to take away the fear.

Except this was Max. And Max had never been afraid of anything.

"I don't want to be alone," he finally said. "This isn't some kind of trick or…seduction, heaven forbid. I just… I would like to lie on the floor next to you if you would let me."

"Max, I don't know…"

"Please, Nor. It doesn't have to mean anything. Other than giving me a few hours outside of my head, maybe a chance to actually sleep. I don't think I've slept in so long. And if I can't sleep, then…at least I can listen to you breathe."

"Okay." As if she could refuse him. No, that wasn't the problem. The problem was how much she didn't want to.

He did as he said, settled the blanket on top of the rug next to her bed. A rug she knew was threadbare. He tossed the pillow down, then carefully lowered himself. She could see him taking care with his leg.

It couldn't have been comfortable. The hard floor, thin rug, the hum of pain in his leg. It was unlikely he would be able to sleep.

But he'd listen to her breathe and he made it sound as if, just by doing that, she had given him some kind of gift.

Of course that's what it must be for him. He'd stared down his own death and survived. Everything that had happened since the night of the storm was one long gift for him.

She still had trouble trying to imagine it. What had it been like to lie in that raft on the cold, endless ocean? To know his leg was broken, to watch others die around him. To bury them at sea, knowing there might not be anyone left to do that for him.

Eleanor tried to close her eyes against his pain. But it was winding itself inside her, around her heart, and it wasn't letting go.

When Harry had come to tell her Max was gone, she'd spent days wondering how it had happened. Quickly? Slowly? Had he been terrified? Had he known it was happening? Had he drowned? Had he frozen to death?

Now she knew he had been terrified. Knew he'd believed he was going to die.

Except he was Max Harper and he'd found a way to live.

And she was making him sleep on the floor because she was a coward.

"Max, you can sleep with me on the bed. On top of the covers so—"

"I'm fine," he said from the floor.

She leaned over the side of the bed. His arms were over his shoulders, his hands under his head. She could see the outline of his muscles and was again struck by how thin he was.

She'd picked the lasagna because the pasta had been filled with meat and cheese.

A meal that would stick to his bones. It's something Marilyn might have said.

"I mean it. I won't be able to live with myself knowing how uncomfortable you are."

"Believe it or not, this might be the most comfortable I've been in two years."

"Max," she said in a tone he would recognize.

He sat up and they were at eye level. "I didn't want you to think I was trying to weasel my way into your bed."

"I'm inviting you," she reminded him.

"If I was any good as a con man, then I would set it up so that you would invite me, thinking it was all your idea."

"Yes, but we both know you're not that good at subterfuge."

He smiled, and she couldn't help but smile back. It was true. Max was bold, cocky, a crusader and sometimes honest to a fault. Surprises, trickery and subterfuge were skills out of his grasp.

Because every time he picked out a present

for either her birthday or Christmas, one that he was particularly excited about, he always gave it to her early. He could never wait to see her reaction.

One time he tried to plan a surprise party after they were first married. He'd managed to keep it a secret for weeks, then blew it the day of the party, not able to pull off exactly why she needed to stay away from their apartment between the hours of 6:00 and 8:00 p.m.

Eleanor remembered being annoyed with him that she'd been forced to act surprised when she finally came home to everyone jumping out of corners.

Annoyed with him. For being thoughtful enough to want to surprise her for her birthday. It all seemed so petty now.

She moved over to make room on the bed. He dropped the blanket on top of the covers along with his pillow. Moments later, he was on his back, settled, and Eleanor had the thought she had probably made a mistake.

She wasn't going to sleep.

Instead, she was going to stay up all night and listen to Max breathe. Just because she could.

Damn it.

She heard a soft huff. He was nowhere close to falling asleep, either.

"We used to talk like this for hours."

"We did," she agreed. Only now she couldn't think what they could talk about. The past seemed too sad. So did the future really.

"Don't do what you usually did, either."

Eleanor didn't know what he was talking about. She knew she didn't have a snoring problem. "And exactly what was that?"

"Cuddle. You were a cuddler. Big-time. If I wake up in the morning and find you draped all over me like a blanket, I'm going to kiss you."

"Max!"

"I'm just saying don't cuddle or suffer the consequences."

Eleanor didn't exactly put kissing Max and suffering in the same category, but it was bad enough she was sharing a bed with him. Kissing him was simply out of the question.

It's just that he was always so warm. Like her own personal bed warmer. She could always find him during the night as a source of heat. Would he still blaze as hot after so long in the cold? It was hard to know. Not taking any chances, though, she rolled over on her side, her back to him.

"Good night," she mumbled into her pillow.

"'Night, Nor. And…thank you."

She didn't answer because she really didn't think she deserved it. The least she could do was be here for him while he reacclimated to his life. The least she could do was be some company for him in the night. The least she could do was share a bed large enough for them both to sleep without touching.

Right? All those things were the very least she could do.

That's what she was telling herself.

Finally, after what felt like hours, she was able to drift off into sleep.

SHE WAS WARM. So blissfully warm. In her dream she was on a beach and the sun was blazing down on her, and it felt so good. As if she'd been cold for ages and only now remembered what it felt like to lift her face to the sun.

"I warned you."

In her dream she turned her head to see Max in the lounge chair next to her. Which was strange because they had never taken a beach vacation. The only time they had for vacations was usually spent in the cabin.

They should have done that. They should have gone to a beach and drunk fancy drinks with umbrellas and lain out in the sun. Why didn't they do that?"

"Nor, I mean it."

Eleanor blinked her eyes open. She meant it, too, she thought. Beach, drinks, the sun and Max. Except when she opened her eyes they weren't on the beach together. They were in bed together.

Her leg was thrown over his thigh. Her body was pressed up against his side. Her arm was lying across his stomach. She lifted her face, and she could see he was staring at her. His dark emerald-green eyes. Always her favorite color.

"This is your fault."

"My fault?" she asked, still in the haze of warmth and sleepiness.

Then he was bending toward her, and, in a heartbeat, his lips were there. Max Harper knew how to kiss. It might have been the first step of her falling in love with him the first time. When he kissed her, it was like his entire being was focused only on her. As if she was this rare creature, instead of just any other woman he might want to kiss.

He slid down in the bed so that they were eye to eye. His hands came up to frame her face, tilting her head at will for whatever provided him the best angle. Right, then left, until finally she opened her mouth and he was plunging his tongue inside. Deep slow thrusts of his tongue that reminded her of what it felt like to belong to Max Harper in that way.

Because that's what it had felt like. As if all of her life she had been waiting for him so that everything could make sense. It's why his absences always hurt so profoundly. Because, without him, she was lost in a haze of confusion.

It's why she had to leave.

Leave.

Left.

Immediately, Eleanor pulled out of his embrace, her hands pushing hard against his chest. Forcing herself to roll away from him until she was on her feet on her side of the bed.

Max, too, rolled out of bed. On the other side, as if showing her he was deliberately backing away, the mattress an expanse between them. Except, of course, he had been the one to kiss her in the first placc.

"You shouldn't have done that," she accused him. Even as she tried to control both her breathing and the throbbing between her legs.

Max was not unaffected. She could see his erection tenting the material of his sweatpants. Which obviously didn't help the throbbing between her legs because all she wanted to do was touch him. Slide her hand inside his pants and touch him in a way she knew would have him throwing his head back and groaning.

She was nearly trembling with the urge to do just that. Because it was exactly what she would have done before.

Which was why she couldn't do it now.

"I'm not sorry," he said stubbornly. And why should he be? After all, he had warned her. But she couldn't be held accountable for something she did in her sleep.

"I need to…" She didn't know what she needed other than to leave the immediate vicinity.

She didn't want to see his red and swollen lips that were no doubt a match for her own.

She didn't want to see his heavy cock, hard and pulsing for her. She didn't want to think about how it had felt to have him inside her body and what that might feel like again.

She couldn't. If the kiss had shown her anything, it was that she was too vulnerable to him.

Eleanor made her way around the bed and out of the room. There was only one bathroom, and, for now, she was claiming it. She went through her normal morning routine, then turned on the water in the shower.

Cold water might have made more sense to calm her down, but she wasn't a masochist. Instead, she let it heat up until it was almost painful, then she stepped inside and let the water relax her.

Relax her until the bathroom door popped open.

"Max!" she said, immediately turning around so that her back was to him. Not that it still didn't put her ass on full display in the clear glass shower door.

"Nor, I'm sorry. But I have to piss, and then I need to brush my teeth."

"You can wait!" she screeched.

"Please," he said even as she heard the seat of

the toilet go up. "This is you taking a shower. We're talking no less than fifteen minutes."

"I don't care."

"We lived together for three years. What's the big deal?"

She heard the toilet flushing, heard the seat go down, because she'd worked hard to train him in those three years. Then she heard the water running in the sink.

"The big deal is we're not married anymore."

"Uh, hate to break it to you, babe. But yeah, we are." This was said around a toothbrush and a mouthful of toothpaste.

"You're doing this deliberately," she said, getting angry. He was trying to make it seem like nothing had changed. Like he could walk back into her life, into her bed, into her bathroom. Re-creating all the intimacies they had shared before. And somehow, all those shared experiences would re-marry them.

The water in the sink shut off.

"Maybe I am," he admitted. "I told you I was going to fight like hell. I never said anything about fighting fair. This used to be our life, Nor. You can't fault me for wanting it back."

"This used to be *your* life. Mine looked a

lot different. Like, for months out of any given year, I didn't have to share a bathroom. It was mine alone because you weren't there."

"Okay. Okay, I deserved that. I need to…figure this out. I want to do better."

"You can start by getting the freak out of my bathroom."

"Okay. I'm going."

She didn't turn around, but she heard the definitive sound of the door closing. No longer able to enjoy the torrent of hot water, she set about bathing and washing her hair as quickly as possible.

Then she wrapped herself up in towels and sat on the edge of the tub thinking how she didn't want to leave the room. Because he was out there. With his lips and his erection and his easy way of being with her.

Because he was fighting and he wasn't doing it fairly. He'd given her notice.

The only sensible thing was to pack up and leave. But, for whatever reason, Eleanor felt like that course of action smacked of cowardice. As if she couldn't handle a kiss from Max without being overwhelmed. As if the idea that he would brush his teeth while she was in the shower was too much intimacy for her to bear.

She ran a business. She employed over a hundred people. She was the person in charge of, not only her life, but also the livelihood of others. She was not about to be cowed by a man. Any man.

Even Max Harper.

He wanted to fight dirty? Let him, she thought. Because she was determined to take anything he dished out and still leave with her heart intact.

Yes, she liked her broken shattered heart, the one she'd pieced back together bit by bit so that, while fragile, it still held. She liked her heart exactly like that, and nothing he did was going to change that.

CHAPTER TEN

IT WAS HARD to know how badly he'd screwed up. She hadn't left. Whether that was because she knew by taking her SUV that would leave him stranded, or because she wasn't as pissed off as she pretended to be he wasn't sure.

As an apology, he was making breakfast. Eggs and bacon with English muffins because that was what she'd brought. It used to be their Sunday tradition.

Shit. Should he have waited until tomorrow to do this? Was that what she'd bought it for? Their last day at the cabin? Either way, he figured there was enough for two for two days, so he was going for it.

She sat at the kitchen counter staring intently into her phone. Sometimes typing. Either texts or replies to emails, he wasn't sure. It was the traditional freeze-out maneuver, which usually he could outwait, but he was short for time.

"Hey," he began to say, genuinely. "I'm sorry.

I mean it. But I really didn't think it was a big deal. Seriously. It never used to bother you."

That, at least, got a reaction. She set her phone down and looked at him. "Actually, it did."

"What are you saying?"

"I'm saying I never liked when you came into the bathroom while I was taking a shower. I'm slow to wake up, and I like that time in the morning when it's just me and the hot water. You come in and you always want to talk. Even when you're peeing, you're still talking. It's annoying. I never said anything because we only had the one bathroom in the apartment and in Norway, but there it is. The truth."

His jaw nearly dropped. Another thing he hadn't known about his wife. "You're serious?"

"Yes."

He was flabbergasted. "How come you never said anything?"

She shrugged. "It wasn't that big of a deal. I assumed it was just one of those married things a person had to get used to about the other person."

Max used a fork to move around the bacon.

"Is there anything else in the three years we were living together that you didn't like?"

Eleanor sighed. "Max, this isn't about making up some list."

"Isn't it? Because this is important, Eleanor. If we're going to do this going forward, then we should have a clean slate. I want to be a better husband, not the same husband."

"Max! There can't be any— I mean, I'm really struggling to figure out how you think we can have a future together."

That shocked him even more. "You weren't asleep for more than ten minutes before you cuddled up against me. You slept all last night in the very position you'd slept in for three damn years. And when I kissed you, you kissed me like a day hadn't gone by, let alone almost three years. I'm struggling to understand how you don't see a future between us!"

She had no response to that, so he refocused on the task in front of him. A few minutes later, he served her a plate of two eggs over, done well, four slices of bacon and a buttered English muffin with a side of grape jelly.

She looked at the plate of food like she wanted to cry.

"Damn it, Nor. I asked you to come with me to give this a shot. But you never had any intention of that, did you? This was about you humoring me. Wasn't it?"

Playing with the fork in her hand, she started to break apart her eggs. "I came because I thought I owed it to you. This was going to be hard for you. I knew that."

"So that's it, then," he said feeling this gaping pit in his stomach. "You don't have any feelings for me at all anymore."

"Of course I have feelings for you, Max," she snapped. "I'm never not going to have feelings for you. That's just how it's going to be. But you can't come back into my life after being dead for more than two years and think we can just pick up where we left off. Because where we left off was you getting on a boat and me leaving Norway. And don't pretend like that wasn't significant. Because the storm didn't happen on that trip. It happened on the one after that."

He leaned back against the counter and crossed his arms over his chest. It wasn't as if he was hiding it. It just hurt to think about. On so many different levels.

"I told you I had a plan," he finally said.

"So you said," she said, then started nibbling on her bacon.

"You don't believe me. That I was absolutely going to come back for you."

Again, she shrugged. "I really don't know what you were thinking back then, Max."

He'd been thinking that his wife shouldn't have up and left him.

"Okay, yes, I know it was stupid. I should have…come after you right away. But at first I was so damn angry. I didn't think you would leave, and when you did…it felt like you gave up on us. I couldn't handle that. Or I should say, I didn't handle that well. They had extended the funding for another month. I was mad enough at you that I decided to do it. One more month and I would get over how pissed I was, and then I would come home and we would work it out. Somehow."

"That's my point, Max. Even if you hadn't taken another tour of research duty, I don't know that there was any working it out. We wanted different things."

"I wanted you," he said, looking at her, spearing her with his intent. "It didn't take two

weeks more at sea to figure that out. To realize I screwed up. I didn't need almost dying
to understand how important you were to me.
That happened long before the storm hit. You
can believe that."

She pushed the plate of food aside. "I asked
you not to go, and you left. I believe that, too."

"I'm never going to do that again."

Shaking her head, she pulled away from the
counter. "I'm going to go change. I brought
some hiking boots with me. I want to take that
path up and around the mountaintop."

She didn't believe him. Didn't believe, either,
that he could change or he had changed. But it
was still early. He hadn't been lying when he
reminded her of how she liked to sleep. And
that kiss…if she hadn't pushed him away, he
had no doubt it would have led to him sliding
inside her. Just like he had on any number of
early mornings.

It was like they were helpless against it. The
constant pull of their two bodies needing to be
connected.

"Can I go with you?"

Her chin wobbled, and he knew she was
fighting an internal battle. He was counting

on the Gaffney stubbornness to play into his hands. He'd asked for a few days. She'd promised that. That meant them spending time together, not apart.

"Sure," she finally said. "But you should eat first. You need to rebuild your strength."

He liked that. Liked that she cared enough to point that out. "How about you finish your eggs and I'll make some for me, then we can explore the mountain together."

Another shrug as she returned to the counter and pulled her plate closer. "Seems like a shame to waste the bacon."

He kept his expression neutral, but he couldn't stop himself from enjoying the fact that his wife loved his bacon.

She always had.

ELEANOR STOPPED AT the top of the incline before it leveled out and took a deep breath. The pine was so crisp and fresh it nearly overwhelmed her senses. She'd forgotten how much these hikes did for her. The way they cleared out her mind of all the useless things she worried about. Mostly about her and Max. Instead, up here everything was so clear and easy.

Max was puffing hard, the hike clearly a strain on both his stamina and his right leg, but he wasn't quitting.

He would never quit. It simply wasn't in his nature.

It's why, after days on a lifeboat in the middle of a frozen ocean while others died around him, he hadn't died. She'd never met anyone who had Max's single-minded determination. She used to think if he'd wanted to, he could have been a Navy SEAL or a Special Ops operator. He had that kind of mental focus.

He'd just turned all that on his scientific work.

Max Harper had gone on a mission to save the planet, and what separated him from other scientists like him was he actually believed he was going to do it.

It felt like you gave up on us.

It was stunning how hurt she'd been by those words. And if she were honest with herself, how guilty they made her feel.

After she'd left him, she used to rationalize daily why she'd done the right thing.

He'd put their marriage second.

He loved his work more than he loved her.

He'd been incredibly selfish.

All really good reasons to leave a husband. A marriage.

Except he would always go back to that same defense. He'd told her up-front what the first few years of their marriage would be like. He'd said there would be trips away. He said there would be long stretches for him at sea. He'd told her time and time again before they got married that the first five to six years would be tough for both of them.

But she hadn't been able to see it. She couldn't have known what it would feel like to be so isolated from everything she'd ever known.

So she'd quit.

She'd issued an ultimatum, and when he didn't do what she'd wanted, what she'd demanded…she gave up on them. It had always made her feel particularly weak, when she liked to consider herself a strong woman.

"Oh, sweet mother of all that is good in this world, please say we can take a break."

He'd finally caught up with her on the ridge where the ground leveled out. There were a few large boulders scattered around the path, and he eased himself onto one.

"We can go back."

He lifted an eyebrow. His left one.

"Right. Sorry. No questioning your manliness. Sure, surviving in some remote village for two years with a broken femur might seem tough, but that's child's play to hiking the northern path around the cabin."

"Good to see you still remember that about me."

Eleanor rolled her eyes. "Funny, isn't it, that your worst qualities stuck around the longest. I'm serious, Max. We should go back."

"Don't placate me," he puffed. "I need to be pushed if I'm going to get back into shape."

"You need to not go beyond what your body can handle or you could get sick, which would just set you back."

"Which is why resting is a nice compromise."

"Now I definitely remember that. Max Harper doesn't do compromises. When you compromise, both people lose."

He sniffed as if she'd pointed out something that smelled particularly awful.

"I was an ass. You should have done a better job of reminding me of that."

It was hard, Eleanor thought. To reconcile this older, more mature version of the man he'd been. It might have only been just over two years, but instinctively, she knew it was more than that for him. Like two years' hard time in his own twisted prison.

"What?" he asked.

As if he could see straight through her down to her soul. Something he always used to be able to do. Something she shouldn't want him to be able to do now.

There hadn't been much of her soul to see in the past few years. She'd been more machine than woman. Working endlessly, because it helped to keep her going.

Because Max had been dead.

And now he was alive and she was nothing but feelings, it seemed.

"I still can't believe I'm sitting here looking at you," she said, putting word to her thoughts. "Speaking to you. It catches me off guard, and there are moments I have to wonder if this isn't a very weird, very prolonged dream."

He nodded. "It's how I felt on that island. As

if it was something that couldn't possibly be happening to me. Death… I had reached that moment where I had to acccpt it. Hcll, at one point I'd been in enough pain, could feel myself slowly freezing to death, I actually welcomed it. But that sense of powerlessness, of being alive but not able to get to you…that was crushing."

For a man like him, it would be. Max was a man who liked to be in control.

"I'm sorry, Nor. I'm so sorry I messed us up. Have I said that yet? Not the almost-dying part. I couldn't control that. Or maybe I could have… I should have never gotten on the damn ship in the first place. But before that. I was so damn…cocky. So sure you wouldn't leave. Positive that you would always be there waiting for me when I got back."

"You and me both. Leaving you was the hardest thing I ever did. But I had to do it. It felt like the only way to…survive us. That must seem dramatic, given everything you've been through…"

"No. No, *us* was that big. That dramatic. At least it was to me. If it hurt you…to leave me, then that's a good thing."

"You're happy I was in pain?"

"Yes," he said quickly. "The more you hurt, the more we meant. The better chance I have of proving to you we can be an *us* again."

Eleanor was done arguing the point. She didn't think they had a future. He did. It was an impasse that wasn't likely to change in the next few days.

"Tell me something about yourself. The person you are now. Another thing I don't know."

The question startled her.

"You think I've changed?"

"Of course you have. It's been three years. You suffered the loss of your marriage, the death of your husband, the death of your beloved in-laws. They treated you like you were their daughter."

"They had a hard time…when I came home without you."

"You know that wasn't directed at you, right? Any anger they had was directed at me. The last words I have from my father is a letter reading…and I'm quoting… *Get your head out of your ass and come home to your wife.*"

It was hard to hear, but it actually made her smile. "Sounds like Harry."

Max shook his head and ran a hand over his face. "I can't believe I'm never going to hear his voice again. Mom's."

"I'm sorry," she said, then not even knowing what was driving her, she moved toward him, standing in front of him so that he could reach out and take her hand. It was all she offered him, but it seemed to be enough to get him over the hurdle of his grief in that moment.

He squeezed her hand, then let it go.

"No distracting me, though. Tell me something about you, the new you."

The new her. The woman who had left her husband, suffered his death and tried to build herself into something she could be proud of. Something he could be proud of.

Was that true? Had part of what had driven her all this time been about making his ghost proud?

The ghost who was currently sitting on a large rock in front of her, looking at her as if she was the most fascinating person on the planet.

It was a trap. Another thing he excelled at, really listening to people, absorbing the words, instead of just letting whatever they said roll over him without paying attention.

"Nor?"

She shrugged. "You know about Head to Toe…"

"That's not you, that's your business."

That made her laugh. "No, that is me. I am Head to Toe. When people use the expression *blood, sweat and tears*, that takes on a literal meaning when you're trying to get your company off the ground."

"But you did it."

"I had already failed at a marriage. I wasn't about to go oh for two."

"Stubborn," he said even as he pushed himself off the boulder until he was standing again. She could see him wince in pain as he shifted his weight to both legs. "Just like your mother."

"Yeah, well, I'm not the only one."

"I know. Now let's walk while you talk."

They did, but Eleanor still struggled with what to tell him. When she thought about who she had been back then and who she was today, she didn't think of herself now with the most flattering of descriptions.

Harder. More focused. Less emotional.

Colder to a certain extent, with maybe a smattering of bitterness.

It was why she hadn't even considered dating. She couldn't imagine any man who would want to be around her. She wasn't exactly sure why Daniel had been so insistent. Then again, the company had been its own attraction. He had wanted Head to Toe before he thought about wanting her.

She tried to focus on what she considered to be the more positive aspects of her new life.

"I'm smarter about a lot of things. Less afraid to try things."

"Does that mean I can get you to try sushi?"

"No. Fish is still gross. And thanks to Norway, that hatred has now become more of an ideology."

"What new things have you tried then?"

She thought about something she'd done. A thing she'd tried. She considered telling him. Wondered how it might affect him, affect them. But it just didn't feel like the right time.

"I meant more in terms of marketing the business rather than food choices," she said.

"You're talking about your expansion."

Eleanor nodded. "Last year I never would have had the courage to think as big."

"Nor, you know I'm asking for more than just the kind of businesswoman you've become."

She flinched at that. Because she didn't know if she was anything but the businesswoman she had become. Because she felt defensive, she turned it back on him. "Isn't that what you wanted? For me to find my own thing. My own *passion*. Now you're going to criticize me because I've done that?"

"No," he said quickly. "No, I'm incredibly proud of what you achieved. But you're making it sound like your life for the past three years has been nothing but your company."

"And Daniel," she said. Another wound she could inflict.

"I didn't get the sense he was that important to you."

She shrugged. "I'm probably not going to know the answer to that now. Am I?"

He stopped, but she kept walking. She wanted to leave the guilt she felt at deliberately hurting him as far behind her as she could.

After a couple yards, she stopped and looked back at him.

"Well, are you coming, or are we turning around?"

He tilted his head as if he was studying her. Like some rare aquatic life form that had captured his attention.

Wondering, no doubt, if part of being the new her also meant being a bitch.

He seemed to reach a conclusion.

"I'm going wherever you are going."

CHAPTER ELEVEN

"WHATEVER THAT IS smells delicious," Max said as he came into the living room and turned the corner to see Nor moving around the kitchen like a woman with a purpose. Max had taken probably the longest shower of his life, but the hot water had helped to ease his muscles and kept the throbbing in his leg to a minimum. He'd pushed himself today, and he was paying the price for it, but it felt good.

To challenge his body, to take it beyond where it could go. It's what he'd done for months on the island trying to get himself in shape enough to get off. He couldn't allow himself to forget the journey wasn't done. He would probably have a limp for the rest of his life, but he wasn't going to let his leg sideline him from doing the things he wanted to do.

Like follow Nor on a hike around the top of a mountain.

Even if she was being a bitch.

She's doing it on purpose.

Intellectually, he knew that. But it didn't hurt any less. The idea that she'd become this hardened shell of a woman because of what he'd done to her didn't sit right with him. He knew who she was deep in her heart.

"I'd forgotten how much I actually like to cook."

He took a seat at the island to watch her work. "I guess working every night until seven precludes cooking."

She muttered her consent even as she popped two potatoes wrapped in tinfoil in the oven.

"What can I do to help?"

She gave him a look. It was her are-you-serious face. He'd seen it a million times and in a million ways. Any time he suggested something he knew she would refuse. There had been a time, during those days spent lying on his back wondering if she'd moved on with her life, found someone else, when he used to think he was never going to see any of her expressions again.

Here, now, it almost brought him to tears. He coughed and turned his head to avoid her gaze.

"I know I'm not the greatest in the kitchen,

but it's because you wouldn't let me be," he said. "You never let me help."

"You're saying that, in all the time we were together, you wanted to do the cooking?"

"No, but I can change that. I can get better at it if I need to. I mean, there are cookbooks. Surely I can read one of those and turn the ingredients into actual edible food."

She cocked her head. "Why this sudden desire to learn how to cook?"

"Because your business obviously requires long days. If I can have dinner put together and waiting for when you get home, I figure that has to be a plus."

She looked at him like he was crazy. "You? Are going to cook? Dinner? For me?"

"I'm sensing a certain level of disbelief. I guess I deserve that, but I don't think you understand how serious I am, Nor."

"Max, you can't possibly think that having dinner waiting for me when I get home is going to fix us."

"Fine. Then what will?"

Another sigh. "How about we put a pin in that conversation? Instead, we should talk about some of the practicalities. Like your parents' estate."

"I definitely don't want to talk about that."

"Max...it has to be done. Your parents didn't have a ton of savings, but the house was worth a small fortune when it sold."

They had loved that house. Bought it cheap in an upcoming area just outside of Denver and had lived there all their lives, so it was completely paid off.

"It's all sitting out there in an account. I thought about donating it to a charity, Save the Oceans, in your name."

"Keep it. You said you were out on a limb financially. Use that money to help."

She shook her head. "I can't. It's not right."

"Is something burning?"

There wasn't, of course. A control freak like Nor would never allow anything beyond the desired outcome when she put her mind to something. It was just an easy way to change the conversation.

She stopped talking about money, checked that all of her dishes were at the perfect temperature, then grabbed a bottle of wine and set it in front of him.

"Fine. You win. No more talking about money. Open, please."

He did as directed and poured them both a glass of some deep, rich red, which tasted better than anything he could remember.

Except his wife's mouth.

The kiss had been good. He needed to find a way to get back to that. Then he remembered what he needed to tell her. The promise he'd made to himself when he thought about these few days together.

It was a risk. He knew that. He'd wanted to get them on better terms before he brought up any of this shit, but she wasn't giving him many opportunities to actually work on their relationship.

After dinner, he told himself. It would be soon enough.

THE MEAL HAD been fabulous. He hadn't expected anything else. Some combination of chicken and spinach and artichokes with a loaded baked potato. A hearty meal, a healthy meal. Something she knew he would love.

Yes, she was doing everything she could to keep him at arms' length. But when she dropped her guard, he could actually feel the caring touch that had always been part of Nor.

They were sitting in front of the fireplace, her back in her solo chair while he felt miles away on the couch. They were already on their second bottle of wine, because there wasn't much to do in the cabin but talk and drink and play games. Neither of them, however, were in the mood for cards.

"I have to talk to you about something." There, he thought. It was done. There was no going back now.

"That sounds ominous," she said as she sipped her wine, her eyes fixed on another fire he'd successfully built.

"It could be. I don't seem to be making much headway in convincing you of my intentions."

"Max, I don't have any doubt of your intentions...it's the outcome that seems crazy to me. We couldn't make it work—"

"Because I was selfish."

"So what does that mean? You're going to spend every day for the rest of your life doing whatever I want?"

"No. But I'm going to spend every day not

taking you for granted. Not taking what we had for granted."

"What did you want to tell me?"

The words clogged in his throat, but he knew it had to be done.

"I cheated on you. When I came back and you were gone... I told you I was angry. At you, at the work, too. We were a week out to sea and one of the other scientists had smuggled a bottle of whiskey in her carry-on. We got drunk, and it happened. That's when I knew."

ELEANOR HEARD THE words and knew it was up to her to ask the next question.

Knew what?

Except she didn't. Because as much as it hurt to hear it, to know he'd been with another woman most likely to spite her, she also experienced a profound sense of relief.

"I cheated, too," she whispered. "I wish I could say it was after...well, after you were supposed to be dead. That would have made it morally unequivocal I suppose. It was after the four months, when you didn't come back. I had just started the business. I flew to San Francisco to meet with another woman who

had opened a similar concept who was willing to mentor me. I was alone at the bar of my
hotel. He bought me a drink. I thought it would
prove I was moving on with my life. It was the
first time I had done anything like that. A one-
night thing with a stranger."

She watched him swallow, saw his Adam's
apple bob in his throat. "Did it? Did it prove
that?"

Eleanor shook her head. "No. It didn't prove
anything."

Other than it hadn't been sex with Max. It
hadn't felt like being with him. It had been
awkward and strange and eventually she faked
her orgasm just to get the guy to finish it and
leave.

Then she'd sat in the shower stall for what
might have been hours sobbing as water rushed
over her.

"What did you know?" she finally asked him.

"I knew I never wanted to be with another
woman again. I knew I had screwed up big-
time. And I knew I would move heaven and
earth if I had to, to get you back. I knew all of
that before the storm hit. Before I saw death."

"And her?"

"She didn't make it off the ship. I tried…but she was scared and panicked and convinced herself that staying was better than going, even though there was no question it was going down."

"I'm sorry."

"Me, too. She was a good scientist. I was sorry for them all. And at the same time there was this sense of disconnect. Like they weren't people I knew and worked with and ate with. Like they were apart from me somehow. I'm sure some psychologist would have an easy word for it. Disassociation maybe? All I knew was that feeling was the only way I could cope with what happened. Did you ever…see him again?"

"No. My first and last one-night stand," she said, not trying to hide how awful she had found the whole experience.

"And since then?"

She shifted in her seat, uncomfortable with what the revelation might say about her. "I was starting a business, Max. It's not like there was a lot of time for casual dating. There was also the fact that you had died. I was allowed to mourn. Wasn't I?"

"Nor, I'm not calling you out because you didn't sleep around. In fact, I'm pretty damn pleased you didn't. Maybe that makes me a caveman, but I'm sorry. If that guy from the hotel walked through that door, I would punch him the face. Okay."

"Yeah, well, if that *scientist* walked through the door…" She stopped herself when she heard how ridiculous it sounded. The poor woman was dead.

"It says something, Nor. About us. That even though you left, even though you thought I was dead, there was something keeping you from moving on to the next thing."

"Yes. My company," she insisted. "Which I was beginning to realize was a problem, which is why I agreed to go out with Daniel. I want to have children…or wanted to. I don't know anymore. That path that seemed so set in stone shifts daily now."

"The path is here. We can get back on it if we want to."

"How?" She winced. She shouldn't have even asked the question. Asking the question might give him hope. Asking the question might give her hope.

"Let me move in with you when we get back to Denver."

She gave him a look.

"Okay, that might be rushing things. What about dating? I'll take you for coffee, we'll eventually upgrade to dinner and a movie. We did it once before. We can do it again."

Dating. Max. The first time had been such a whirlwind. She'd fallen so hard, so fast she hadn't once thought to pull back. To protect herself. There had been boyfriends in high school, guys she hung out with and dated in college.

There had been no one like Max.

He'd whisked her up, and she'd been happy to go along for the ride. Marriage made sense. Not waiting made sense. Leaving with him to go to Norway…made sense.

Until none of it made sense anymore.

"How did you feel when you came back to find me gone?" she asked him.

He held up his hands. "I felt gutted. The anger was there, yes. But I felt as if the world wasn't solid under my feet anymore."

It sounded right to her because that was exactly how she'd felt when she'd gotten off the plane in Denver.

"Why would you want to go through that again?"

He set his glass on an end table and got up from the couch. He moved toward her, but she had no idea what to expect until he sank to his knees in front of her. Grunting a little as he shifted his weight, he slowly rested his hands on her thighs and looked at her.

"How did it feel when you were with *him*?"

She shook her head. "I don't want to talk about that."

"And I don't want to hear it, but you asked me a question, and I'm asking you. Honestly, tell me how did it feel. I'm not talking about the physical stuff. I'm talking about the moment it was over."

"Wrong," she whispered. "Just so wrong. I didn't know if it was the guilt or..."

"I know," he said shaking her thighs. "I know exactly how it felt, because I felt it, too. Losing you hurt more than I could possibly imagine. And maybe no one signs up for that kind of pain twice in one lifetime. But seeing you again at the party—your face, your eyes—

looking at you again and knowing I was standing in the same room as you brought me more joy than I thought I could ever feel. So, yes, I'm willing to take the risk."

It was easier for him, she thought.

"You've already lost so much… How can you tell the difference between wanting to try again and wanting to hold on to the last thing you knew before your world was upended?"

"I told you, because I knew that I had to win you back. I had to find a way to fix us before that storm ever hit. Everything that happened… that was all about making me wait for it."

"Max…"

"Date me. Let me prove that I'm a better man or at least that I'm willing to work at being a better husband."

"I need to think."

He smiled at her. Brilliantly.

"Why are you smiling?"

"Because you thinking is better than you believing all of this is crazy."

"My ex-husband came back from the dead. Trust me when I tell you I think all of this is crazy."

"Your husband, Nor. We're still married.

That knot we tied is still as strong as any bow-line knot I've tied in my life. I'm certain of it. We hurt each other. We can choose not to do that and move forward together."

She huffed. "See, this is what it's like. To be under the Max spell. You, on your knees, saying everything right, making it sound like it could be again what it was."

"It can. I wouldn't put you through this if I didn't think that was possible. I made you happy."

"You made me miserable, too!"

He nodded in concession. "I know, but I made you happy. Really happy."

"I always wanted a big wedding," she blurted. Because she couldn't think of any other defenses she might have.

He leaned back on his haunches. "Come again?"

"I always wanted a big wedding. When I was a girl. I wanted the dress and the flowers and the cake. I would get cupcakes for my birthday and I would make Allie practice with me as we fed them to each other, but really we would smash each other in the face with them. I wanted all of that."

"You said that was your mother's idea."

"It was," Eleanor admitted.

"You said you didn't need any of that."

"I didn't need it. I just wanted it."

"Is this like the bathroom thing?"

"My point is I wanted what you wanted, Max. I would have done whatever you said, because I was that much in love. Giving up my girlish ideas of a wedding with all the trimmings seemed like the easiest sacrifice to make. Giving up my dreams of starting a business so that we could move to Norway for your research was a snap. All of it had been so easy for me to do, but when we fought that last day—when I told you I would leave—you told me I should get a job. That I should have my own thing that I was passionate about besides you. I let you overwhelm me. Me. Eleanor Gaffney. And then you stopped liking who Nor Harper became."

"No," he said pushing himself to his feet even as he grimaced through the pain. "Never that."

"Admit it, Max. The reality is if that storm never hit, if you came home and your parents were alive and happy, you would have given me the divorce, and we would have gone our separate ways."

He looked at her, and she could see he was angry.

Then he took a breath and ran his hands through his hair. Maybe a sign of resignation.

Of giving up.

It's what she wanted. That's what she told herself.

Then slowly he shook his head. His eyes still on the fire.

"Kiss me again."

"Max…"

"No. You said what I'm feeling is a condition of my grief. Prove it. Kiss me. Every time I have ever kissed you, I knew we were it. I won't lie to myself, Nor. If I can kiss you and not feel that…whatever *that* always was, I'll know it."

Eleanor rolled her eyes. "Great, you'll know it. But what about me?"

He smiled in that charming, almost disarming way he always had about him. That smile that suggested sometimes he didn't have all the answers. Which made him infinitely more human. More fragile.

More vulnerable.

"I'm selfish. I get it. Please, give me this. If I fight the war and lose, I can live with it. If I'm fighting, like you're suggesting, for the wrong cause, then that's not fair to either of us."

She stood before he could stoop to his old tactics. It would always start with a request, then turn into a taunt, finally a challenge. Something her pride would not allow her to back away from.

And the truth was she wanted to know how it would feel, too. This morning hadn't been a fair test. She'd been sleepy and not in her right mind. Aside from three glasses of wine, which left her slightly buzzed, she was still of sound mind.

He wasn't wrong about whatever...*that* had been. That magical something that went beyond physical pleasure and had become as addictive as any habit she could possibly imagine.

In short, Max Harper had been her heroin.

She'd forced herself to kick the habit—an accomplishment she'd been proud of at the time.

But wasn't the real test of recovery to see if she could be tempted again and still resist?

"Fine, you want to kiss? Plant one on me."

He laughed. "Plant one on you? What are you, my grandmother?"

She put her hands on her hips in clear, defiant challenge. "I don't know, Max. You seem pretty cocky that you can kiss me and figure out the answers of the universe as pertains to us. I'm thinking you might want to rock my world in the process."

"Nor Harper..."

"Eleanor Gaffney," she corrected him.

"Not yet," he whispered even as he stepped closer to her. "Not quite yet. But if you want your world rocked, then who am I to back off from that?"

It was then that Eleanor realized she might have miscalculated. As he stepped up to her and surrounded her space. When she could smell the hint of the soap he always preferred, still fresh from his shower. When she looked into his eyes that could see right to bottom of her soul.

Max had been her drug. Her downfall.

And maybe three years of recovery hadn't been anywhere close to enough to getting over him.

CHAPTER TWELVE

SHE USED TO like it when he cupped her cheek. She used to like when he rubbed his thumb along her jawline. She used to like everything he did. Or so he'd believed.

"I like holding your face in my hands when I kiss you. Do you like that?"

She nodded.

"I never asked you any of those things," he whispered as he pressed a soft kiss against her lips. "I always just assumed…"

Her fingers circled his wrist. "Max, I didn't hide everything from you. Not when it came to this."

"I didn't think you could hide anything from me period."

He kissed her again, another gentle press of his lips against hers. Feeling the fullness of that bottom lip which always drove him so bat shit around the bend with lust. He needed to compartmentalize his feelings. Sex and feeling good weren't the issue. It was the other feelings that had always been layered under the physical goodness. Like a special dessert that wasn't just sweet or rich but something else. Something more substantial.

He wrapped his hand around her neck and brought her close up against his body. He'd always loved the feel of her, and now it was like, suddenly, he was hungry again.

He hadn't felt like this. Not in three years. Not even all the days spent on the water, he'd been in too much pain for that, too cold for that. On the island they had fed him as much fish and fish eggs as any man could stomach. He'd never once recalled being hungry despite dropping so much weight, which had been more a result of the diet and his lack of appetite than anything else.

No, *hungry* wasn't the word. He was *ravenous*. For the feel of her hair sliding over his fingers, the soft skin of her face under the stroke of his thumb. Her lips, her tongue. Her taste.

He needed it all. It was the only thing that made him feel alive. The only purpose for getting out of that forsaken village. This, his wife. Not that, the stranger on the ship when he'd been so damn furious. Not any woman who had ever come before Nor.

Only her.

"Nor," he said pressing his face against her neck, trying to control this insistent need to take her to the floor and slide his cock deep and hard inside of her. As if he could fuse their two bodies together. Making a new thing. A statue of two lovers entwined made of actual flesh and bone.

This was not grief over the loss of his parents. This was not grief for the lost two plus years of his own life.

This was simply the thing he'd always known to be true. From almost the first moment he saw her.

"I missed you. I missed you so damn much," he cried. It wasn't in him to stop the tears that he could feel dampening her shoulder. She was here, in his arms, and he could smell her and feel her and taste her.

He was alive again.

He was in love again.

"I love you," he choked out.

She pulled away. As if the words burned her.

"Don't," he pleaded.

But she was shaking her head, looking at him like he was a ghost.

His jaw tightened with frustration, but he could acknowledge that he'd pushed her too hard. Too fast. Again.

His problem was that he'd given her an out. A few days to convince her they should be together. All she had to do was get through these days. Max was honest enough with himself to admit he hadn't thought it would be this hard to convince her.

Nor had loved him, and he wouldn't let himself believe that had changed.

It was the fear that was holding her back. Fear of him hurting her again.

Fear was a feeling that could be overcome.

"I'm not going to apologize for saying it," he said. "I do love you. I have every day we've been separated."

"I can't...it's too much. Too fast."

"That's always been our problem, hasn't it? Everything has always happened so fast for us. What if we slowed it down?"

She tilted her head in that way she did when she thought she was getting played.

"What do you mean?"

"I asked if you wanted to date. Why don't we do that? Why don't we take time to get to know each other again? We can put off the divorce—"

"You said a few days. You said if I came with you, you would give me what I want."

"And you want a divorce?" he asked, his throat closing around the word. "Is that what you really want?"

She crossed her arms over her chest and wouldn't look at him as she nodded.

"It's the only thing that makes sense," she said, repeating her words from earlier. Like there was logical order of things that happened when a man came back from the dead.

"I suppose. Then again, love doesn't really make sense. Does it?"

"I—" She pointed over her shoulder toward the bedrooms.

"Got it. You want to escape."

She jutted out her chin but didn't contradict him.

"It's okay. I'll stay up. Make sure the fire goes out."

"Uh… I don't want you to be… I mean, I don't want to leave you…"

She was worried about him again.

"I'll be fine, Nor. I won't bother you again. This morning and just now made you uncomfortable."

She flinched at the word. Nor never did like to be told what she felt.

"Good night," she said tightly.

"'Night."

He should have let it go at that. But as she walked away from him, he knew he couldn't.

"I felt it again, Nor. What you need to consider, judging by your reaction to that kiss, is that I'm pretty sure you felt it, too."

He braced himself for whatever lie she might tell, but she clearly couldn't even bring herself to do that.

"Good night," she said instead.

ELEANOR STARED AT the ceiling of her bedroom. Dawn was happening outsidc. This big, huge planetary event and she thought about what it was going to bring.

A drive home. Leaving Max.

Never seeing him again.

For the second time in her life.

It might have been easier if he hadn't been

so damn right. When he kissed her, it was so easy to get lost in it. So easy to feel the pull that was the Max gravity. Once upon a time, it had sucked her into a big deep hole that she'd had to crawl her way out of with her heart in shatters.

Now he was threatening to bring her back to that place.

The place where she'd been loved and cherished. Until he took her for granted.

When she'd left him, everything had been colored by the pain of the separation. When she thought he was dead, everything had been tainted by grief.

She didn't think she had ever actually looked at their relationship for what it was.

But that wasn't really what he wanted her to do, was it? He wanted her to look at what they could be.

Max wanted to date. Max wanted to make her dinner when she worked too late.

Max wanted to kiss her.

"Ugh!" With a growl, she rolled out of bed, unable to deal with the mess that was in her head right now.

Her life had been simple. Work. And work. There was her mother and her sister. There was the mild complication of Daniel. And there was more work.

Now she'd been plunged headfirst into the plot of a bad soap opera, and she didn't know how to get herself out of it.

Other than to leave.

She rubbed her chest even as she made her way to the bathroom. Max's bedroom door was open, and she peeked in, unable to help herself. Had he left the door open on purpose? Maybe that had helped him to sleep, she thought. Maybe having the door open made him feel closer to her.

How wrong had it been to deny him the basic comfort of company?

No, she couldn't think about that. Worrying about Max was a step away from caring about Max, which didn't feel too far away from falling back in love with him.

Forcing herself from his doorway, she went about her normal morning routine. The shower cleared her head and made her focus on her next priority which was coffee, then convincing Max they had to head to Denver as soon as possible.

Another day wasn't going to help her situation. It was only going to make things muddier.

When she was dressed and feeling a little more in control of herself, she walked into the living room only to stop when she heard the soft sound of his breathing.

Walking around the back of the couch, she saw that he'd fallen asleep there last night. Still dressed, no blanket. It was chilly without the fire, but he obviously didn't feel it.

How cold and alone were you? On a raft in the ocean...dying.

Did you think about me?

Eleanor felt a sob escape her throat before she could control it. There, lying on the couch, was a living, breathing Max Harper. Suddenly it was real to her in a way that it hadn't been before.

As if she'd truly believed she'd been dreaming this whole time, only she wasn't.

Max was alive. And she'd spent the better part of their time together being a complete and total bitch to him because she was so damn afraid.

"Hey, it's okay."

He'd woken up. He must have heard her.

Or felt the tears that were running down her cheeks and dripping onto his arms.

Instead of getting up, he pulled her down on top of him. He was there, underneath her. A little leaner, a little bony, but still her Max.

And she continued to cry. Even as he rubbed her back and made that shhhing noise she knew was something his mother always did. She buried her face in his neck and just let herself cry. For him. For her. For their marriage. For his parents. All the grief that she hadn't realized had been stuck in her chest for years.

Sadness she'd carried around because she had to.

She rubbed her face on his shirt, not caring what she left there, and when she lifted her head, she could see his eyes. So warm, so full of that spark that had always captivated her attention.

Eleanor didn't think about what she did next. She didn't think about the ramifications or how it might hurt later. She only knew that Max was alive and she could see that life in his beautiful green eyes, and she wanted it.

She wanted to take it inside herself and revel in it.

Bending her head, she took his mouth. If he was shocked by her sudden change of heart, he certainly didn't let it deter him. His hands were in her hair, her hands were sliding up his shirt until she could feel the beat of his heart against her palm.

He turned her so that her back was against the couch, and they were facing each other.

This time his eyes said something else. Something that was dark and delicious and made her stomach drop.

He bent to take her mouth again, brought her leg over his hip and pressed his entire body into her.

God how she had missed this. Touching and feeling and bodies connected. That awful one-night stand had felt so awkward and wrong, there had been nothing enjoyable about it.

This felt like something old and familiar, but at the same time, thrilling and new. She reached around his back and ran her fingers along his spine. Then she was shoving them into his jeans so she could feel his ass and remember what it was like to have Max Harper fully belong to her.

"Nor… I can't… I need…"

She couldn't hang on to his words. They were floating above her head while she relearned the things she used to know about him. That her nails in his ass cheeks drove him wild. That if she found a certain spot on his neck with her teeth, he would groan.

His hands were between them pulling down the leggings she'd put on until she could help him kick them off. Then his fingers were there, inside her panties, stroking her, pushing her past desire. She was already so hot and slick.

"Honey, please. I need you so bad. Tell me you want this as much as I do," he said against her lips even as he continued to play with her.

Yes, she thought. She needed more than his fingers. She wanted the thrill ride that always came any time she'd made love with Max. It was like riding on a motorcycle, or coming off the downside of a roller coaster. Sometimes it was slow and deep and intense. Sometimes it was fast and furious as if they couldn't help themselves.

"Yes, Max. Now. I need you inside me."

He pulled his head back and looked at her. "You mean that? You want that?"

She nodded. Of course it was what she

wanted. She was this raging ball of fire, and he was the only thing that would satisfy her.

He hooked her one leg high over his waist then he moved his hands to his jeans. She heard the sound of the zipper, felt the press of his cock against her panties; then there was a tearing sound that told her, her panties were no longer an issue.

With one heavy full thrust, he was buried inside her. It stung for a moment, not having been filled like this in so long, but then she tipped her hips toward him and suddenly they were once again like a lock and key.

"Nor," he grunted. "You feel so damn good."

She had no reply. There was nothing but the feel of him between her legs, thrusting hard and heavy. Belatedly she realized he had his hand under her top, rolling her nipple through the satin of her bra.

"Baby...I need you to come for me fast." He pressed his forehead against hers even as his hips continued to snap against her. "I can't... I can't wait."

Except she wasn't thinking about coming, she wasn't even thinking about the jolting pleasure that kept shooting through her in waves. All she was thinking about was the feeling of him deep inside her, pulsing, alive. It was something she never thought she would have again. A feeling she would never experience again. She was giddy with it. She pushed against him, desperate to take in more of him.

"I can't... Sorry, Nor. I have to...sonofabitch!"

He slammed into her, like he had no control over his body, and it was joyous. She could feel herself explode from the inside, and the pleasure was unlike any orgasm she'd ever had. It kept rolling through her, like a sharpness that should have hurt, if it didn't feel so incredibly good.

Then it was over. She could hear the harshness of his breath against her ear. Could feel the pounding of his heart against her chest, between her legs. He was still inside her, and she wrapped the leg that was around his waist even tighter so that he would stay that way.

"Babe, I'm sorry. That was over too soon, but...three years is a freaking long time."

She ran her fingers along his jaw. "Yes," she whispered against his lips. "It is."

He laughed then and she laughed, too.

"Next time, we can do it slower," he said. "I promise."

Next time. As if *this* time was the start of something.

That was the sucky part about spontaneous, out-of-your-mind sex. When it was over and you realized what happened, you had to deal with all the ramifications of what it meant.

Like the feel of Max sliding out of her body. The gush of wetness between her thighs…

"Holy shit!" Eleanor sat up even as Max was tossing her leggings over his head and trying to settle back on the couch with her.

"No," he complained as he tried to pull her down with him. "I want to snuggle. You know me, babe."

Then she pushed him with enough force that sent him falling off the couch.

"Hey!"

"Sorry…" she offered lamely, as she started doing the math in her head.

"What's wrong?"

"I'm not on the pill anymore. That's what's freaking wrong. And you didn't use a condom."

"Nor, I haven't used a condom with you since the first few times we had sex."

It was true. She'd been on the pill, they were in a steady, monogamous relationship. There had been no reason. Except she'd stopped taking the pill because...stupidly it made her sad to take a pill every day to prevent something that could never happen because she wasn't having sex.

She'd had her period almost three weeks ago. She could be erratic but, for the most part, she was fairly regular. Which meant she should be out of the danger zone.

There were options of course.

But as soon as the day-after pill came into her mind, she rejected it. There was no reason to panic. It was one time. She should be getting her period in a week or so. No reason to take any drastic measures.

"I need to go home," she said suddenly.

"Nor, we need to talk about this."

"There is nothing to talk about. This was a mistake. I was emotional and vulnerable." She said this even as she pushed the long top down to her knees.

"Hey...that makes it sound like I took advantage of you. That is not what happened here."

Eleanor looked at him. His jeans were still

undone, and she could see his still semi-hard penis. Part of her wanted to sink to her knees and take him in her mouth; the other part wanted to run.

"I wasn't blaming you. I was trying to explain my own motivations. It was a weak moment. It happened. We need to move on."

"What the hell are you talking about? I don't know if you realize it or not, but we nearly set the couch on fire. I haven't come like that—check that. I've never come like that."

"You said…two years."

She was pulling her torn panties out of the crease in the cushions when Max grabbed her by her upper arms, forcing her to meet his gaze.

"That had nothing to do with time. That was us. That has always been us. Why are you being so damn stubborn about this?"

"Max, you can't fix everything with sex! Yes, it felt good. Yes, we have chemistry, but none of that was able to keep us together last time."

"Last time I kept leaving you. This time I'm not going anywhere!"

Eleanor shook her head. She couldn't have this conversation while not wearing panties.

"Please," she said, knowing it sounded like begging, but having no other choice. "Please, I just need to go home."

He opened his mouth as if to argue but seemed to think better of it. There was nothing he could say that was going to take away the sudden panic she was feeling.

"Okay."

The relief moved through her. So profound she felt the tears well up again.

It was that sense of reprieve, of knowing that he was backing off that made up her mind.

Max Harper was the worst kind of Kryptonite for her. And the only way to deal with Kryptonite was to get as far away from it as she could.

CHAPTER THIRTEEN

"I CAN'T BELIEVE we're fighting about this," Allie said, even as she was cutting the tomato for the salad she was preparing.

"I can't believe you can't believe we're fighting about this," Mike fired back.

Allie shook her head. "What is the big deal? You know how Mom is. You know she has to have that feeling of control at all times. This is just her doing her thing. If you're going to get upset every time she does—"

"No," Mike said. "That's not what this is about and you know it. Stop deflecting."

There were times she really hated him when he called her out on her shit. She was about to continue to do what he accused her of doing, when the doorbell to their home rang.

They stopped and looked at each other. When you lived on a farm, it wasn't like you had visitors dropping by casually to see you.

"Did you invite anyone over?" Allie asked.

Mike shook his head. "I'll get it."

Allie rinsed her hands off. As she left the kitchen, she could hear voices in the foyer.

One of those voices being her sister's.

"Eleanor," Allie said as she made her way through the living room to the foyer. First, it was Thursday night, which meant a work night for Eleanor. Second, if she was in North Platte, she wasn't in Denver. And third, Allie couldn't remember when Eleanor had actually taken a day off work.

Then she remembered the trip with Max.

"What is it? What's wrong?" Because the only reason for Eleanor to be here had to be because of some tragic event.

"Can I stay here...for a few days?"

Allie's jaw dropped. "You want to stay in Nebraska? For a few days? While Head to Toe is in Denver?"

Eleanor pointed to the laptop case she had slung over her shoulder. "I can work remotely."

"Eleanor, is this about Max? What happened at the cabin?"

Then her sister did something Allie hadn't seen in three years. Tears filled her eyes, ran down her cheeks even as she tried to brush them away and her chin wobbled.

Eleanor's chin always wobbled when she was upset because, Allie knew, she was fighting every instinct in her body to not cry.

She nodded, and Allie pulled her inside to the living room. The house had been Mike's parents' place before they retired to Florida, so the furniture was old and lived-in. Something Allie wanted to start changing as they made this more their home rather than his childhood home. But as nearly everything they had was going into the wedding, there was little left over to replace what was still functioning furniture.

Allie sat with Eleanor on the old couch and looked at Mike.

"You need anything from your car, Eleanor?"

She nodded, and Allie could see the relief cross his face. Allie had no doubt he would take the longest amount of time a human could fetching whatever Eleanor had in that car.

"There is an overnight bag…in the back seat. I'll need to wash some things…"

"No problem. I'll be back."

"Talk to me."

Eleanor put her face in her hands and started crying again. After a few minutes of back rubbing and sympathy, Allie tried to press her.

"Tell me what happened. Was it awful? Did you two fight?"

Eleanor nodded, then tried to take a few deep breaths to get herself under control. "I don't know why I'm crying. It was my decision. My call. I should feel relieved but instead…"

"From the beginning, Eleanor. So I have some context."

"Max wants us to stay married. He wants to just pretend these three years never happened. No, that's not fair. He says he wants things to be different. He says he's different…but people can't change. Not really. That's what Mom always said."

"Not even people who have near-death experiences?" Allie pointed out.

Eleanor glared at her. "I knew you would be on his side. But I had nowhere else to go. He doesn't know about Mike's farm. He won't be able to find me here."

"First, I'm on your side. Always. Second, I've never known you to hide from anything."

"I'm not hiding," Eleanor insisted. "I'm just…

lying low. I called my attorney. She's updating the divorce papers now. I think…he'll be a little shocked when he receives them. Which is why I should not be where he can find me. Not at work. Not at Mom's. And I—I didn't want to be alone."

Allie heard the front door open.

"I'll just put your things in the guest room," Mike called out, then took the stairs without bothering them. Another escape tactic, Allie thought. Really, men and tears. What was their deal?

"Why is Max going to be shocked?"

Eleanor winced.

"Eleanor," Allie urged. "There's no point in holding back. Not with me."

"I told him I needed time to think. I didn't know what else… I needed him to back off, and it was the only thing I could think of. He probably thinks there is still a chance for us… but I can't. I just can't go back there."

Allie nodded, sensing they were finally getting closer to the truth. "Does he think there is still a chance because you made it obvious you still have feelings for him?"

Another scowl.

This time she stood and paced the floor in front of Allie.

"Feelings aren't enough. Passion isn't enough."

"Passion? Eleanor, did you have sex with Max?"

The answer played out on her sister's face.

"Hookay."

Eleanor snapped at her. "Don't judge me."

Allie held both hands up in surrender. "I'm not judging. I'm just trying to put all the facts together. You went away with him, you still have feelings for him, you had sex with him—"

"And now I'm divorcing him," Eleanor finished.

"Yeah, not exactly the conclusion one would arrive at. You have to see what's happening here, Eleanor. You're scared and you're running."

"Of course I'm scared. This is Max! I have to completely shut down any and all emotions when it comes to him and think only in terms of what letting him back in my life would mean."

"That's not happiness?"

"Allie!"

"What? Eleanor, I've obviously known you all my life. The happiest you've ever been was when you were with Max. And the most miserable you've ever been was when you left him. After he died…or we thought he was dead. You weren't even you anymore. What happened—him being not dead—it's a freaking miracle. A second chance that you probably shouldn't have gotten. I understand why you're scared. I just don't understand why you're rushing to make everything so final. What's the hurry?"

Allie waited for a response. Eleanor had stopped pacing, but it was strange because Allie couldn't remember a time when her sister had looked so defeated.

"You don't understand," Eleanor said dully.

It was true. Allie didn't. For one, she couldn't imagine ever losing Mike. But if she'd lost him and suddenly he was back… That had to be playing mind games with her sister.

"Okay. You're right. You need me to be supportive Allie right now."

Eleanor looked at her as if she'd been granted a lifeline.

"Yes. Please."

Allie nodded. "You got it."

"You're sure Mike won't mind if I stay a few days."

"I don't mind if you stay a few days," Mike said as he came into the living room. "But you should know Allie and I are fighting."

Allie rolled her eyes. "We're not *fighting* fighting."

"We're not agreeing, that's for damn sure."

"What?" Eleanor asked.

"Mom," Allie answered as if that explained everything.

"See, that's where you are wrong," Mike said, obviously frustrated. "This has nothing to do with your mother."

"What are you talking about? You're pissed because she made decisions about the wedding without asking us first. I told you...that's just what she does."

"I'm not pissed because she booked a band and then told us about it after the fact. That's vintage Marilyn. I'm pissed because you don't even *like* that band, and you still won't say anything to her about it. This is our wedding, *your* wedding. And you're going to dance around to a band you think sucks because you can't stand up to your mother."

Allie bit her lip. He was right. When her mother had told her what she'd done, she'd been furious. Listening to her rattle off about how she was getting a steal and someone else wanting that day so she had to act fast, and the whole time Allie had been thinking *no*.

No, she didn't want that band.

No, her mother shouldn't have done what she did.

No. No. No.

The word had been in her head. She just couldn't seem to get it out of her mouth.

Eleanor raised her eyebrow.

"Oh, no. Not a word out of you. You're running away from your back-from-the-dead husband because you're scared. You don't get to lecture me about my mommy issues right now."

Mike shook his head. "Allie, I love you. I'm going to marry you no matter what. But if you don't figure this shit out with your mother, I swear it is going to build up inside you. It'll feel and taste like resentment, and it will ruin the relationship you have with your only living parent."

"What Mike said," Eleanor agreed. "Because

let's face it, between the two of us, she actually likes you. It's only fair that she has a good relationship with one of her daughters."

"Fine. I will do this. I will tell her that I do not want that band. Eventually. In the meantime, I'm just going to cancel them and pray Mom didn't put a deposit down."

"That's the passive-aggressive woman I know and love," Mike said with a smirk.

Allie stuck out her tongue at him.

"Now, if you're both done giving me shit, I'm sensing Eleanor needs chocolate ice cream and lots of it."

"I thought we were having a big 'healthy' salad," Mike said.

"Can you please stop saying *healthy* like it's a bad word. I'm trying to inject vegetables into your diet. This is not a crime."

"I always had to hide them with Max," Eleanor said, really to no one. "Put them in things so he would barely notice. Like the spinach. He probably didn't even realize I had stuffed the chicken with it."

Allie looked to Mike, and he seemed to immediately understand.

"I'm thinking you're going to want some whiskey with that chocolate ice cream."

"Yes," Eleanor whispered. "I think I'm going to need exactly that."

TWO DAYS LATER Eleanor was sitting at the kitchen table cursing the single monitor on her laptop. If she were sitting at her desk in her office, she would have two monitors and, in theory, be doing twice the work.

As it stood, she was keeping up with emails, but, in the long run, this was not sustainable. She needed to be in her damn office.

And of course, she would be if she weren't such a coward.

Her lawyer had sent a courier last night to the hotel where Max was staying to serve him with the divorce papers. Eleanor figured he might try to track her down at the office today, maybe try and wiggle a phone number out of Selena. Although at last check with her number two, he hadn't been in contact.

His last option would be to call Marilyn. Except Eleanor knew her mother would not give out any information to him. Marilyn seemed to be on her side when it came to Max. Which was strange.

They were never on the same side.

As if she'd summoned her, Eleanor heard the back door open and her mother call out with her usual, "Hellloooo?"

Shit. This was going to require an explanation.

Her mother glanced around and immediately spotted her, even as Eleanor stood to greet her.

"Eleanor, for goodness' sakes, what are you doing here?" It took her mother a few seconds to think about how odd her appearance really was. "Why aren't you working? Are you ill? Why didn't you stay with me if you're ill?"

"I'm not sick, Mom."

Then it was like it suddenly all made sense to her. "This is about Max. You're back from the cabin, except you're here instead of at work, which is very much not like you."

Eleanor winced. She could hear the faint echoes of *I told you* underneath his name.

Marilyn put her handbag—which always seemed to be ridiculously big, every season—on the counter with a sigh. Then she began opening kitchen cabinets like she lived there instead of Allie, and pulled out two mugs.

"I'm making tea, and then we'll talk about it."

Eleanor plopped into her chair. "I don't suppose I can say I don't want to talk about it."

"No."

Right. Who was she kidding?

"Where is Allie?" her mother asked.

"In town picking up groceries. Mike is out in the barn."

"And you've been here how long?"

"A couple days."

She'd literally driven Max to her office to drop him off, then straight to Allie. Calling her lawyer on the way, of course.

Eventually, Marilyn set a mug in front of Eleanor, and, oddly, it was almost as soothing as the whiskey Mike had fed her.

Marilyn took a seat at the table and, in that formidable way she had, demanded Eleanor start speaking with nothing more than two raised eyebrows.

"There is nothing to tell. He wants us to stay married. I want to move on."

"And you're here because…"

"Because my attorney served him with divorce papers last night. I thought it would be easier if I was out of town when that happened. I didn't go to you because...well, Max knows your house."

"I take that to mean he didn't know what you were planning on doing when you left him."

Eleanor shook her head.

"So you're hiding."

Eleanor took a sip of her tea. "If you want to call it that."

"Since when did you become a coward?"

"That's not fair, Mom. You said yourself, I shouldn't have gone with him to the cabin."

"Yes, because I feared it would tie you in knots, which clearly it has. It's one thing to end it before it starts. It's something else entirely to run away from something once it's started. He was your husband, Eleanor."

"I know that! You can acknowledge my situation is complicated."

Marilyn nodded. "And complications should be dealt with head-on. Are you certain you want to divorce him?"

"Yes. No. Yes. Uh! That's the problem. I have this idea that we could have this second chance. That I could believe everything he's saying and we could have all the positives of our marriage back without any of the negatives. Then I think about the real world and how people don't change. He hurt me, and the likelihood is he'll hurt me again. The logical sensible solution is to end it now."

Marilyn blew out a slow breath.

"You think I'm wrong?"

"I think, unfortunately, your father and I weren't the best example as far as marriages go. It's not something I ever thought I would bring up…of course, people didn't speak of such things back in my time. You just pretended like nothing happened, and you moved on. I wasn't very good at that."

"Mom, you don't have to…"

"No. Your sister called me out about it the other day. She was right. Your father and I weren't happy. He cheated on me."

"Oh, Mom. I'm so sorry."

"Yes, I am sorry for telling you. It's not that I want you to think ill of your father. He was a good father to both of you girls."

"Was it a one-time thing?"

"No. It was a woman he worked with. It lasted for a period of time. I found out about it and gave him a choice. His mistress or his family. He chose us, and I believe he honored that commitment until his death, but what had gotten lost in all of that was how I felt. I was angry. I was humiliated. And the truth was, after that...I didn't love him anymore. Yes, he was my husband and the father of my children, and we needed to stay together for the sake of all of that...but I wonder. If things had been different, or like they are today, we could have gotten a divorce, shared custody. Maybe found someone else along the way. I regret not doing that. For both of us."

It was strange, Eleanor thought. Such a sad story, but in that moment, she felt connected to her mother in a way she'd never felt before. Marilyn would probably humph if Eleanor said anything, so, instead, she sipped her tea and tried to extrapolate the moral of the story.

"So you agree. Divorce makes the most sense."

Marilyn shook her head. "You weren't listening. Divorce made sense because I didn't love your father anymore. It wouldn't have made sense if I had. You spent two days with Max, and your gut reaction was to run from him. I think that says something about the state of your feelings."

"I thought you were on my side," Eleanor complained. "You never liked Max."

"Oh, Eleanor, don't you get it? I'm your mother. I'm *always* on your side. Whether you can see it or not. And it's not that I never liked Max, it was that he was as headstrong as I was and I knew how you battled me."

"It might be too late," Eleanor said, shaking her head. "The petition…he's not expecting it. It will hurt him that I did it without talking to him first. He thinks…he thinks we still have a chance."

"Hmm. If he thinks that, then doesn't he?"

Eleanor didn't know how to respond to that, so she didn't.

"Hey!" Allie announced coming through the back door with two bags of groceries. "Mom, this is a nice surprise."

"Is it?" Marilyn asked, and suddenly Eleanor knew she was no longer in the spotlight of her mother's attention. "Why did I have to learn, and not from my daughter, that she had chosen to cancel the band I arranged to play at her wedding?"

Allie busied herself with putting away groceries and not looking at her mother. "I was going to call you. I was."

"Hmm."

"Allie, just tell her the truth," Eleanor encouraged her.

Allie, apparently, had other ideas.

"Mom, Eleanor is hiding from Max who she obviously still has feelings for, but served him with divorce papers anyway."

"Nice try," Marilyn said sardonically. "That ground has already been covered."

"She doesn't like the band," Eleanor said. It seemed like such a simple thing to do. She would never understand her sister's reluctance to be open about what Eleanor considered minor decisions. "It's her wedding and she doesn't like the band. You shouldn't have booked it without asking her."

"Well, I know that, there wasn't time. Why didn't you just tell me when I told you what I had done?"

Allie shrugged.

"Two cowards," Marilyn said with disgust. "It seems I've raised two cowards. Allie, next time just let me know if you don't like something I've done. It was embarrassing to take the call from the booking agent, not realizing you had canceled. They were very nice and refunded my deposit. Eleanor, you have a company to run. Hiding out at your sister's place is a disgrace to Max, yourself and intelligent, independent women everywhere. Get off your butt and deal with your problems. Can people change? That's what you wanted to know? I did. I changed. If only I'd had the courage to follow through with it, both your father and I would have been a lot happier."

Marilyn then picked up her teacup, put it in the sink, grabbed her oversize handbag and left without another word.

Allie looked at Eleanor. "Well, I hope you're happy. See how you've upset her."

"She's right," Eleanor said flatly.

"I know. I really hate that," Allie agreed.

"I have to go back to Denver," Eleanor said, more to herself than her sister. "I'll go pack my stuff now."

"Good luck," Allie said. "And you know when I say that I mean good luck for Max."

CHAPTER FOURTEEN

ELEANOR DROVE TO her building that Monday morning after a long and miserable weekend waiting for the other shoe to drop. Except Max hadn't called or found out where she lived. Maybe he'd been so angry about what she'd done that he was done with her?

That thought shouldn't have made her so miserable. She pulled inside the garage and parked in her usual spot. She'd already spoken to Selena on her way to Denver. She knew that Max had, in fact, stopped by the office on Friday afternoon. He'd been polite and gracious. Simply asking where she was.

Selena, of course, told him nothing.

"Did he seem angry?" Eleanor had asked her, even as she clutched the phone in her hand so hard she feared she might break the case.

"No. But he did seem sad. Maybe even a little defeated. I'm not going to lie. I felt sorry for the guy."

Of course Selena would. It was rather a sad story to tell. Happily married couple splits up because the wife can't handle her husband being away for long stretches only for him to almost die, do everything in his power to find her, then get served with divorce papers a few days after his miraculous return.

It sounded heartless to Eleanor, and she was the woman in question.

She got out of her SUV and hit the locks. It was only as she made her way to the elevator that she saw him.

"I know. This is creepy as hell, but I didn't have any other way of finding you, and Selena wouldn't let me wait upstairs," Max said. "And I didn't want to do this over a phone call."

This was it. This was about confronting her problems head-on. Except seeing him again, all she could remember was the feel of him between her legs, the smell of him, the taste of him.

The rush of him.

This man who had made her feel so loved. As if fairy tales existed and she'd been selected as one of the lucky princesses.

Divorcing a man like that...some would consider it impossible.

Eleanor lifted her chin. "I was a coward to do it the way I did it. I apologize for that."

"I thought we left things with…you would be in touch. I thought you were *thinking* about things."

"I did think. And I was in touch, just by courier," she said, then winced. "It was easier to do it from far away."

This time it was Max who sighed. "Doesn't that tell you anything, Nor? Doesn't it say something to you that you're so freaking uncomfortable around me you had to run away?"

"I'm willing to admit that, but it doesn't change my mind. In the end, the thing that makes the most sense…"

He rushed forward. "Stop saying that. Stop saying that we don't make sense. Not when you're the only thing in my life that's ever made sense to me. Say you stopped loving me. Say you don't want to be with me anymore. Say that. But stop talking about us as if we're this business problem you have to solve."

Eleanor felt every single one of his words like they were knife jabs into her chest.

Stop loving him. Was that even possible?

"What are you going to do, Max?"

"Do?"

"You can fight it, I guess. Plus there is my company at stake. Colorado isn't necessarily a fifty-fifty state—"

He closed his eyes. "Please stop talking. I don't want your money. I don't want your company. I don't want to fight you. I wanted to fight *for* you. I lived for more than two years with a single thought in my head that I might be lucky enough to have a second chance with you. I guess I got that chance. That's all I can ask for, really."

"Max…we could— Maybe we don't have to not be in each other's lives. Maybe we could try and be friends…of a sort."

He laughed, but there was no humor in it. "No, you were right. If we try to become something else, we'll never move on from each other. You wanted kids someday—"

He stopped talking, and now Eleanor felt like crying.

"It hurt too much, Max."

He nodded. "I guess some things you can't fix."

"What will you do now?"

"I meant what I said. I'm not going back to

research or field assignments. University of Denver has offered me a job. I'll take that, find a place and settle down. You're okay with me staying in Denver?"

She wasn't. She had fears that she would spend her days looking for him. At a coffee shop or a restaurant. At some point, she might see him out on a date with another woman.

There was a delayed sense of pain. She remembered the woman he'd gotten drunk with, the one he'd had revenge sex with, and suddenly she wanted to hit him really hard in the arm. For the drunk woman and any woman who would come next.

But of course, she couldn't. Because she was making the choice to let him go. She had no claim on him anymore.

"We still need to talk about your parents' estate—"

"I told you, I don't care about that."

"Max, it's not just the money. I have to turn over the cabin to you, too."

He flinched then. "That cabin was my parents'. It was us. I don't want the damn cabin. Sell it."

That hurt, but she supposed it was her due.

She'd held on to the cabin to hold on to a piece of him. Now she was being offered all of him, but she was choosing to walk away.

"Max…"

"No. I get it. I'll contact your lawyer. Give her all my information. That way…that way we don't have to do this again. You're right about that. It hurts too much."

Eleanor's chin wobbled, but she nodded.

"I'll let you get back to work."

She watched as he walked away, and she held back the scream in her throat. Then he turned and gave her a salute with his two fingers. "Have a good life, Eleanor Gaffney. Please try and be happy."

She couldn't respond. She couldn't actually form any words. Instead, she turned and hit the button on the elevator that would take her up to her company. Her office. This thing that she'd built that would never love her the way Max Harper did.

It would also never hurt her the way he did.

One month later

ELEANOR SAT AT the table wondering why she'd agreed to lunch. It seemed a simple enough thing. A few weeks after she'd filed for divorce from Max, Daniel had called her. They'd had a casual conversation. How was she doing? How was the expansion going?

Was she still with Max?

No, I...we...decided divorce was the only option.

Then he'd said they should get lunch sometime. Catch up. Lunch had sounded infinitely less threatening than dinner, so she agreed.

Two weeks after that he'd called to make it an official date.

Now she was sitting at the table alone, thinking it had been a mistake, while he was in the men's room.

What if Max walked in? What if he saw her on a date with Daniel? Would Max recognize Daniel from the engagement party? Would Max wonder if Daniel was the real reason she had pushed for the divorce?

That couldn't be good, she thought. Being on a date with one man, while obsessively wondering what her soon-to-be ex-husband would think.

It had been a month, and there still wasn't a day when she didn't have doubts about what she'd done. Of course, there also wasn't a day when she didn't think she'd made the smartest decision she could.

The one that protected her heart.

If it was so protected, why did she feel like shit most days?

A question she didn't think she had a good answer to.

Daniel came back and sat, resettling the napkin on his lap. "So, have you decided what you want?"

"The cobb salad looks good," she said, still going over the menu as if it were the most fascinating book she'd ever read. Looking at it was easier than looking at Daniel.

"Eleanor," Daniel said smoothly. "It's very good to see you again."

She lifted her head and smiled. "You, too."

"And your family? How are they? Still in the throes of the wedding planning?"

Yes, Eleanor thought. The wedding was safe territory. "It's still a battle between my mother and my sister. My mother winning most of them. They've moved from the band and the flowers to the wedding dress. I'm supposed to head down in a few weeks to be the deciding vote between what they have picked out."

"Shouldn't that be Allie's vote by herself?"

"It should," Eleanor said. "The worst part about it is that it seems all Mike and Allie do anymore is fight about the wedding. He wants her to stand up to our mother. She wants him to be more supportive. This should be an exciting and fun time for them, but it's…well it's not."

"That's a shame."

"Yes," Eleanor agreed.

"However, if they do manage to pull this off, it sounds like you'll still need a date. I'm more than happy to put my name in the ring."

For some reason her heart froze at his words. It was like she had to tell it to start beating again. To start breathing again. The wedding was months away. If she brought Daniel as her date, that meant they would have been dating for almost nine months.

That would mean a relationship. She wasn't ready for a relationship. She'd barely been ready for one when she thought Max was dead.

"Daniel…"

"I rushed that," he said even as he winced.

"You've been very kind and very patient—"

"Patient and kind," he interrupted. "Two things a man never wants to hear himself described as when vying for the affections of a woman."

"There is nothing wrong with being kind," Eleanor grumbled.

"No, but it seems as if women prefer the type of man who takes action. Which of course, I thought I was doing by inviting you to lunch. Maybe you needed more time to get over your not-so-dead husband."

Eleanor fidgeted with the silverware on the table, lining it up more evenly.

"I'm sorry, Daniel. I thought… I don't know. I thought this would be a way to move on, but I guess I'm not ready."

He nodded thoughtfully. "No, it wouldn't seem that you are. Not if the idea of going to a wedding with me is enough to rob you of breath. You know, many women think I'm a charming fellow."

Eleanor smiled, because she knew he was trying to lighten the mood. "I have no doubt."

"But it appears that our romantic future is not to be. I can't tell you there isn't a ping of regret, but I do understand."

"Thank you."

"Then we should probably move off the topic of our relationship and move on to another topic entirely."

Eleanor couldn't imagine what he meant. She was actually hoping he would ask for the check, pay for their two iced teas and call it for what it was. A horrible third date.

"What topic would that be?"

"Your company, of course."

"Oh. Well. Things are going really well. As you know I'm a little overexposed with the expansion, but so far we've seen pretty good growth."

"Yes. I know. I've been following it. But I think it's time to look beyond your capabilities and think bigger."

"My capabilities have gotten me where I am today," she said, trying not to be defensive. Obviously, Daniel had more success in the world of business. He'd made a fortune investing in companies at just the right time. She wasn't dismissing any of that. She'd just chosen to grow on her own rather than give up what she considered was hers and hers alone.

"Oh, yes. I know. Please don't think I'm diminishing what you've done. But I've told you together we can do more."

"Together?"

"Professionally, of course. I'm not going to tell you I hadn't hoped we could mix business with pleasure. But now that pleasure seems to be off the table, I think it's time we focused more on the business."

Eleanor straightened in her seat. "I thought I made myself clear. I'm not interested in your investment capital. Not at the cost of one quarter ownership of my company."

"Oh, that's fine. I'm actually not interested in one quarter anymore. Actually I would like half."

"Half! In what universe would I give you half my company?"

Daniel pulled the napkin from his lap and set it on the table. He took a sip of his iced tea, then pulled from his wallet some bills which would more than cover the check and the tip.

"I should have been more forthcoming about what this lunch was about. While dating would have been enjoyable, my ultimate goal has always been your company. You are uniquely primed right now, with my intervention of course, to take your business from being a nice local operation to something global. When I find these little gems, I tend to be very aggressive. Not patient at all, you see."

No, Eleanor didn't see. The Daniel she thought she knew had been reasonable and, yes, kind and patient. This man was...ruthless.

"Well, it's mine," she said stupidly. "You can't have it unless I give it to you."

"That's true. But you're exposed now with your contractors. A man with means could make things...well, we'll say difficult for you. I don't want to do that, Eleanor. I want to help you. You have to see that."

Eleanor stood. "I think I see plenty. Thank you for making yourself crystal clear."

Daniel stood, as well, shaking his head. "Please, Eleanor. Don't be upset with me. This is what I do. This is how small ideas become big ideas. I want to do this with you together."

"And it doesn't mean anything to you that I don't?"

He bowed his head as if he was genuinely upset. "I'm sorry. I can't let an opportunity like this slip by. You're good, but you're just not ready for the big leagues."

Eleanor gritted her teeth. "And if we had dated? If we'd been dating all this time? If there wasn't the *ghost* of Max Harper in the way? What then?"

"Well, I would have hoped, by now, that we would be mutually…satisfying each other. But make no mistake, Eleanor. I would still have taken half your company."

It was then Eleanor knew she had to leave because she feared she was going to become violently sick.

CHAPTER FIFTEEN

SELENA HANDED ELEANOR a washcloth. It was blissfully cool and felt wonderful when she rolled it up and put it on the back of her neck.

"I thought I was nauseous as a reaction to what Daniel was doing but I must be coming down with the flu."

"Hmm," Selena muttered.

The two women were in their own bathroom adjacent to their offices. A bathroom that was just for their private use. A place where either of them could escape to if they needed five minutes away from the eyes of the rest of the employees on the floor.

Eleanor had purposely designed the loft with this in mind. She figured if she ever found out the business was failing and had to tell Selena, who had been with her from the beginning, she wanted to do it in private.

After two years she hadn't thought that was a concern anymore. Eleanor had gotten back from lunch, given her employee a quick rundown, then told Selena to meet her in the bathroom. Before Selena got there, Eleanor promptly lost the contents of her stomach.

She thought back to the last time she'd been sick. When she'd seen Max again for the first time. Apparently her stomach had issues with major emotional shifts in her life.

She'd come out of the stall to find Selena holding the cool washcloth.

There was a bench seat, and Selena took her hand and led her to it. Right before Eleanor's legs gave out.

Bent over, her elbows on her knees, the next thing she knew Selena was pressing a cold glass of water in her hands.

"Slow sips," Selena said as if Eleanor were capable of anything else. Then she sat down on the bench seat and started to rub Eleanor's back.

"Now tell me again what Daniel said."

"I told you. He wants to buy half the company. Take us global. Which maybe is good. Maybe I'm being too narrow-minded. Maybe that would be a good thing for everyone. More jobs, better pay—"

"Stop," Selena said. "Stop thinking about that right now. If you don't want to sell him half your company, he can't make you. It's privately owned. It's not like he can buy up your shares and push you out."

Eleanor tried to think through what he actually threatened. "He said he could make things difficult with our subcontractors. Which he could. We're overextended, and, while we're growing, it's going to take us a few years to pay back all of our loans. What if we lose our packing service, or our delivery service? Heck, what if he just finds a way to take our idea and do it without us, but on a bigger level that would crush us? Hey, Uber, it's me, Lyft, calling. Watch your back."

Eleanor took another sip of water.

"Right now it's just threats. He didn't say specifically what he was going to do. This was just his opening salvo."

Eleanor nodded. "Good point. He probably wanted to see how I would react."

"Then it's a good thing you saved the vomiting for later." Selena nudged her shoulder.

"Selena, this is not funny. This is *my* company. It's the only thing that's given me any focus for the past two and half years. I don't want to share it. I don't want someone else to make it bigger. I want to be the person who does that. I mean, if I'm not running Head to Toe, then who am I?"

Selena took the glass from her hand, mostly because it was shaking so much the water was splashing out.

"Okay, now let's talk about that problem. Which I think is the real reason you are in here having a mental meltdown. You've dealt with shipping delays, poor product quality, losing employees, firing employees, space problems, technical problems. All of it. And through all of that I have never once seen you lose your cool until today. You know what you haven't dealt with very well. Your dead husband coming back to life."

Eleanor groaned. "Please, Selena. I cannot think about him right now."

"Yes. You don't think about him. You don't talk about him. But don't think I haven't come into this bathroom and heard you sniffing like you were trying to stop yourself from crying. And don't think you *not* talking about him to me, your closest friend, hasn't been the loudest thing you've never said. I was here that day, remember?"

The day Harry came to tell her about Max.

Selena shook her head, seemingly lost in the memory of that day. "I don't think I have ever seen somebody so distraught. I remember thinking, and don't be angry with me, well, there goes that job. Because I had never seen a woman, who took a hit like that, get back up on her feet. There was no way I thought that you could deal with the grief you were dealing with and make this company a success. But you proved me wrong. You got up on your feet and you plowed ahead, and I thought, in some ways, it was kind of sad."

"Sad?" Eleanor questioned. "Shouldn't it have been uplifting?"

"Maybe. If you had found a way to be happier. But the work didn't make you happy, Eleanor. It just made you determined. You've been that way every day since—like you have something to prove. To your mother, to Max's memory, to everyone out there on that floor, I think. And you did it. Only now Daniel issues some vague threats about taking what's yours, and you're in here hiding like your world is about to come apart."

Eleanor wished she could say that was a slight exaggeration, but it was how she felt. Like she was a house made out of straw and the big bad wolf was coming to blow her down. She nearly trembled at the idea of how vulnerable she felt right now. A feeling she absolutely detested.

"You know what I think?" Selena asked.

"I know you're going to tell me whether I want to hear it or not."

Selena smiled, but it was the kind of smile someone gave a friend when that friend clearly could not see the thing right in front of her face.

"I think you loved Max Harper with everything you had, and when he disappointed you, that crushed you. But that wasn't the thing that took away your happy. Him dying changed you. Changed how you thought about your life. Now he's not dead, and I don't think it's caught up with you yet."

"What?"

"When you left him, did you think he'd come for you?"

Slowly Eleanor nodded.

"Hmm. And what did you think was going to happen when he did? Did you think you were going to throw divorce papers in his face, and it was going to be over? Or did you think you two were going to have a knock-down, drag-out fight? And that he was finally going to have to see the marriage from your point of view? It's just me. Your friend sitting with you in the ladies' room. It's more sacred than a confessional. You can tell me the truth."

Eleanor bent over and dropped her face into her hands. "I thought...I thought we would fix it. Because I couldn't imagine my life without Max Harper as my husband."

"Which is why you didn't push the divorce back then."

"I was trying to get a company off the ground," Eleanor explained. "I was a little busy."

"You were trying to build something so that when he came back he was going take a look at it, and think how impressive you were. Then he didn't come back, and Head to Toe became your shrine to Max Harper."

Eleanor shrugged. "Maybe."

"My point in all of this... Max did come

back. He came back for you, Eleanor. He was just a little late in getting here. So instead of shutting him out, instead of hiding from him, instead of pushing him away, instead of losing your shit over some asshole making threats at you, why don't you go deal with what's really bothering you? Go have that knock-down, drag-out fight you thought you were going to have two and half years ago."

Eleanor let out a whoosh of breath. She couldn't deny it. Deep down, she really had thought Max would come for her. If she believed him, he'd already made the decision to do that when he got on the boat again.

"It's too late. I hurt him too much by not even trying."

Selena stood. "A man thinks of nothing but getting back to his wife for two years, and you think in one month he's forgotten her and moved on?"

Eleanor rolled her eyes. Obviously Max hadn't forgotten her. But wanting to open himself up for another chance when she'd already shot him down pretty hard? Was that even possible?

"Are you ready to hear something else?"

"No," Eleanor grumbled. "Yes."

"This is not the first time in the last few weeks where I've seen you turn green in front of me. This just happened to be the first time you couldn't control it."

"I said it might be the flu."

"Hmm."

Eleanor looked up at her friend. "What is that supposed to mean?"

Selena shrugged. "Maybe nothing, but I've been sharing an office and a bathroom with you for more than two years, and, like women do, we're usually on the same cycle. I've had my period this month. Have you?"

Eleanor didn't have to think about it. She shook her head tightly.

"That's what I thought. I'm wondering, then, if maybe there isn't something else you're not telling me."

Eleanor sat there knowing there was no point in denying it. She knew what happened at the cabin. She knew she hadn't had her period. These sudden bouts of nausea were happening more frequently, but other than that, she felt fine. No fever or aches to indicate the flu.

She looked up at her best friend and said the

words she hadn't let herself even think. Because it was too surreal that this could be happening.

"Max and I had sex, and he thought I was still on the pill. Only I wasn't. And...I didn't take the day-after pill because...because..."

"Because you didn't," Selena said knowingly. "Go find Max. Go have your fight. See where that takes you. Then we'll deal with Daniel."

"What if he doesn't want me back? I was such a bitch to him," Eleanor whispered. That fear lingered. He'd hurt her so bad she'd been afraid to give him another chance. If she'd done the same to him, could she really hold that against him? And what if she was actually pregnant? God, she couldn't even let herself think that.

Would he believe she was coming back to him for any other reason?

"Two years," Selena reminded her. "But first, I would stop at a pharmacy and make sure you know the truth before you see him. Because that is going to be one hell of an explanation."

IT WAS JUST after nine in the morning. The first rush of students had already gotten their morning coffee, so the small shop on campus was pretty empty when Max stepped through the door. He had class in another hour, but for now he planned to have a latte and read a book.

The reading helped take his mind off Nor. Despite having been separated from her for the last two years, the past month being without her had been that much harder.

Because he knew she was in Denver. Knew she was working behind her desk in her office. Knew that, if he wanted to, he could go see her again. Except, of course, he couldn't.

That would make him a creep and a stalker, and he had no plans of being either. He just wished he hadn't been so smug in the idea that she would eventually realize she still loved him. What they had wasn't something that went away. She'd admitted as much. But if he'd known how scarred she was, how afraid she was of getting hurt again, he would have bargained for a better deal.

Something along the lines of two weeks in the cabin and then he would consider divorcing her. Or maybe two months.

As it stood he still had the divorce papers at home, sitting on a desk. Untouched and unsigned. He'd told her attorney he needed time. Time to settle in Denver, find a place, find an attorney of his own to review the summons. The truth was he was just stalling for time.

Time for Nor to change her mind. Only as each day passed, the fear started to creep back in. The fear he'd lived with for at least a year. That she would have already grieved him and now move on with her life. Find someone else, start a family. All things he knew he wouldn't be able to overcome.

Now he was starting to think her reluctance to give him a real chance was also something he couldn't overcome.

There was small comfort to be had in knowing she wasn't pressing for the divorce. There was also some comfort to be had from the fact that he'd seen a shot of Daniel on TV the other night going to some big-time, celebrity charity event downtown.

There had been another woman on his arm.

A tall blonde who wasn't half as interesting to look at as Nor was, but Max thought it was a good sign she hadn't gone back to dating the man she had been seeing.

The girl behind the counter handed him his

drink, and Max took a seat in the back. Coffee. A book. Like every other joy in his life, something he'd taken for granted.

He heard the door to the shop open, but he didn't look up. It wasn't until he felt the presence of someone approaching him that he lifted his gaze...and froze.

Vaguely he wondered if there was ever going to be a time when seeing her didn't take his breath away.

Nor looked different today. Tired, a little disheveled in jeans and an old T-shirt. Nowhere close to the boss lady in her suit of armor. She had dark half circles under her eyes as if she hadn't been sleeping, and there was a faint tightness to her lips that he took as a sign of discomfort.

There wasn't an expression on her face he hadn't memorized.

"Hi, Max."

"I know why you're here," he said, thinking about the papers on his desk. No doubt she'd come to call him out on his stalling, but it still didn't take away from the fact that she'd come to see him. Could that mean there was hope?

She certainly didn't look like this past month had been any easier on her.

"I doubt that," she muttered. "Can I sit?"

"Sure. Don't take this the wrong way, you know I always think you're beautiful, but are you feeling okay? You don't look well."

"I'm…fine."

"How did you know where I was?"

"I was on campus and got your schedule. I knew you had a ten o'clock, and I know you used to like coffee to chill out before class. We used to come here all the time when we were dating, so I took a chance."

She was right. It had made it harder coming back here. Where they had so many memories, but in a strange way it had given him some contentment, too. Like there was and always would be a connection between their lives.

"Why aren't you at work?"

"Because I wanted to talk with you."

Talking was a good thing. Talking in person was something she didn't have to do. She could do that through her lawyer. Still, the way she'd left things between them he didn't want to get too excited. The split had felt permanent. In truth, he'd been crushed, and it wasn't an experience he was looking forward to repeating.

"About the divorce?" he asked. Ready to launch into a detailed explanation of why it was taking him so long to sign the damn papers.

"No," she said, but then seemed to fidget in her chair.

"Can I get you something? A coffee…"

"No. No, thank you. Uh, maybe…a water?"

"Sure." There was a water cooler set up on a table where the napkins and stirrers were. He filled a paper cup and brought it back to her. And watched as she took tiny sips.

"Seriously, Nor. What's the matter?"

"I'm a little nauseous is all. The water helps."

"Are you sick? Is it the flu?" Was it something more serious? The thought struck him, and it was like he'd taken a bullet to his heart. "Nor. Tell me what it is. Now. You're scaring the shit out of me."

Thoughts of cancer and chemo flew through this brain. Was that the reason she hadn't wanted to give him a second chance? Because there was no second chance for her?

If that was the case he would find a doctor and make one.

She took a deep breath, and he knew that whatever she said next was going to change his life.

"I'm pregnant."

He was right. It did.

CHAPTER SIXTEEN

THE BREATH RUSHED out of his chest. And it took him a few seconds to truly believe it. But it's not as if she would lie about something this important.

"Say it again," he demanded.

"I'm pregnant."

"You said it was probably bad timing," he said slowly. Not sure what uncharted waters he was wading into. Was she happy about it, sad? She was telling him about it. So it wasn't as if she'd planned to terminate the pregnancy.

"I guess it wasn't."

He nodded, taking it in. They had gone to the cabin, they had made love, she was pregnant, and now she was telling him.

"Why do I feel like there is another shoe to drop?"

Nor looked at him like he was crazy. "You want *another* bomb handed to you? I just told you I'm pregnant with your kid."

No, he didn't need another shock. But he was still confused by what it all meant. His instinct was to pick her up, put her in his lap and rub circles on her lower back until she didn't feel sick anymore. Then he wanted to take her back to his place and make love to her so that she would feel incredibly good instead. Then he would tear up the divorce papers, and they would stay married, have a family and live happily ever after.

He just knew it wasn't going to be as simple as that.

"Let's start with the basics. I assume you want this baby." She'd always wanted a baby. As angry at him, or afraid of him as she might be, he didn't think there would be any circumstance where she wouldn't want to keep the baby.

She nodded.

"So we're going to be parents." That felt good to say. Like suddenly there was this whole new connection that had just formed between them. There was no way from this point forward that they weren't going to be part of each other's lives.

If he hadn't thought it would have been incredibly immature, he might have made a fist pump. He was that giddy with happiness.

"I take it that means you want to be a part of the kid's life?" she asked him.

"Of course," he said, a little shocked at the question. Shocked in general by what was happening. "I've always wanted a child with you. We were going to discuss it when I came back…"

Her lips thinned. Max knew it probably was not the best idea to remind her of the fight they had before he left. He reached across the table and settled his hand over hers.

"Nor, I have done everything wrong. Wrong when I left, wrong when I came back. But this is you and me, and we're going to have a baby. Something we both wanted. There is a whole lot of right in that."

She nodded slowly. "I don't really know where to go from here."

"Move in with me. Or I move in with you. It doesn't have to be…it doesn't have to be about us getting back together. But it does have to be about me being allowed to take care of you while you're pregnant."

She didn't immediately say no. Max thought that alone was a victory.

"I don't know, Max. This all seems so sudden—"

"Have you missed me? Not in the past two plus years, but in the past few weeks? Has it been harder for you knowing you might run into me in a damn grocery store someday?"

She nodded.

And there it was. The hope he was trying to contain.

"Okay," he said trying to be cautiously aggressive. "I get this. You thought it would be better to walk away. For a lot of different reasons. But now you're pregnant, and there is no changing that. We're connected. Which means we need to find a way to move forward."

"I agree. But don't you see how this just complicates everything even more? How are you going to know if I want to move forward because of you or for the baby?"

Max took it as a good sign that she was even worried about that. That she was actually concerned about his feelings in all of this.

He wanted a life with her. Any way he could have it. But he knew if he told her that, it would be too much for her to take. A miracle and, well, lack of birth control had given him a third chance with Nor. Something he never thought he would get.

He needed to be smarter about it this time around.

"Then let's not tackle the complicated questions right now. Let's start with you and me sharing some space. Not a bedroom. Just living together to help get ready for when the baby comes."

"Okay. I guess that makes sense. We can just be together and not worry about our relationship per se."

"Absolutely," Max lied. Because he planned to spend every day he had with her convincing her that he could make her happy. That had everything to do with their relationship.

"Okay. I have a condo close to downtown..."

"That works. I just have an apartment I was renting month to month until I decided on something more permanent. Give me your address. After class, I'll go pack up my things. As you can imagine, there isn't much. Then we will just take things super slow. No concern about anything other than making sure you're looked after properly."

"I'm sorry," she said shrugging. "I didn't mean to put you through so much…turmoil."

"If you come with the turmoil, I'll take it."

ELEANOR WATCHED AS Max dropped his bag by the foyer. The place had been new construction a year ago when Eleanor had decided to take the risk on the pricey mortgage. It was just as Head to Toe was beginning to turn a real profit with no end in sight.

Funny, right now she could barely think of the business. She was under a threat from a heavy-duty corporate investor, she'd taken on expansion that was making her vulnerable. Every cell in her brain should have been filled with the company she had started, but instead, all she really wanted was to lie down, maybe have Max bring her some tea, then take a nap.

It's what he'd always done when she wasn't feeling well.

"Wow. Fancy."

It was a nice, modern place. High ceilings. Open floor plan. The opposite of their first cramped apartment. The tiny house in Norway, too, for that matter.

She tried to show him around, but he seemed to get lost in the details. Every picture on her wall he studied. Photos from her life. Some he would remember. Others would be new. He lingered on those even longer.

"This is Selena," he said pointing to the one picture. It had been of the two of them popping a bottle of champagne when they'd passed one thousand customers. It had been a good day.

"Yes. She's really been through it all with me. Not just a great employee but a good friend, too."

"Then I like her."

"I think she kind of likes you, too." Eleanor smiled. "She was the one to convince me that maybe...I had acted too quickly. You know... with the whole divorce thing."

"Then I love her."

Eleanor snorted. "Grab your bag. I'll show you to your room."

He complied and slung his duffel over his shoulder. Funny, it was a sight that always used to make her sad, because it meant he was leaving. This was so much the very opposite of leaving.

She opened the door to the guest room. "The bed should be comfortable. Mom says it is, anyway. The few times she'd been here," she said. "The bathroom is connected through that door. I have my own, so you don't have to worry about walking in on me."

"Because you don't like that," he said, his mouth quirked.

"Correct."

"Have you told your mother yet?"

Eleanor shook her head. "I've just barely had time to process it. I kind of wanted to just have it to myself for a little while. Also, I thought you should really be the first to know. Now I'll tell her and Allie, but it doesn't have to be today."

"Okay."

"I'm not stalling, if that's what you're thinking. I'm just… There is a lot going on right now. With everything."

"Nor, I'm not judging. It's your news to share when you're ready. I'm here only for support. Got it?"

Support. It would certainly be a change for them. When they were married and his work had taken priority. It had been her job to support him until she'd stopped doing that.

She wondered how it would feel to be the one who was supported. She wondered how he would feel taking a back seat to her job. And then she wondered again, what it would feel like to have that support jerked out from underneath her.

So much of what they had done to each other was unfair.

And climbing over that gaping ravine of regret seemed impossible unless you believed nothing was impossible when it came to love. Eleanor rubbed her hand over her belly, thinking about the bean inside. Such a tiny thing right now, but, just maybe, it would be responsible for making miracles happen.

"I'll let you get settled then."

"Yep."

She closed the door behind her and made her way downstairs, wondering if she'd just made the biggest mistake of her life.

Or the best decision ever. Only time would tell.

A FEW DAYS LATER, Max was in the kitchen chopping peppers when he heard the front door open. He checked the clock and saw it was close to eight. Which he supposed was better than last night when she'd gotten home after nine. He was determined not to say anything. He was absolutely not going to be one of those men who didn't understand the demands of running a successful company.

If he was concerned, it was only because she looked so exhausted each night when she came home. To give her a little incentive tonight, he'd let her know he'd picked up groceries for dinner and was going to be cooking. So she texted him to let him know when she was on her way. Everything had been prepped, so all he had to do was toss it in the skillet with some of the garlic sauce he'd picked up and dinner would be ready.

She dropped her purse and kicked off her heels and made her way to the kitchen where he'd already poured her a cold glass of water. It seemed to be the only thing she could drink.

She smiled slowly when she took in his apron.

"Kiss the Cook?"

"If you insist," he teased her. He'd picked the

thing up just for the stupid joke. Anything that might make her smile.

Because the one thing he'd learned in the three days of living with her was that Nor carried the stress of the world on her shoulders. Between him, her job, the baby that was messing with her body and the family she still had to tell, there was not enough plain happy in her day.

Max figured if he was going to have a chance of winning her back, he would need to bring the happy as well as the support.

"I think kissing would complicate things," she said seriously.

"See, and I think kissing would feel good. But since I would need your cooperation, I'll have to defer to your thoughts on the matter."

"Max, are you flirting with me?"

He smiled. "Yes. There was nothing in the rule book about not being able to do that."

Eleanor eyed him warily.

"Why don't you go up and get comfortable? Dinner will be ready in a few."

She cocked her head at him. "You know, you really don't have to cook every night."

He shrugged. "I like it."

"I'm just saying, I know you want to support me, but that doesn't mean I expect anything like this."

"Nor, it's not a big thing," he said, not wanting her to feel any kind of guilt over it. "I like it. I'm home earlier from my classes. Besides, that's my kid you're carrying around. I have a vested interest in keeping you well fed."

He watched as her hand instantly went to her belly. And then he watched that look take her over. One more new expression he got to memorize. A mix of surprise and astonishment. Like she still couldn't really believe it was real. He was convinced that's why she hadn't told her family yet.

Because once Marilyn knew, then it would be very real.

"You really like doing it?"

"I really do."

"And you're not going to resent having to do it night after night?"

"Well, I imagine I'll take a night or two off here and there. If memory serves, you have a weakness for pizza."

She smiled, and it felt like he'd won something.

"Really greasy pizza," she admitted as another smile played around her lips.

"Yes. I know. Double the cheese and the grease. Now go."

She picked up her discarded shoes, and he watched as she made her way up the stairs.

He nodded even as he threw the food into the skillet. This, he thought, was a good night.

A few smiles and a little teasing.

Yes, this was absolutely going to work.

CHAPTER SEVENTEEN

THIS WAS ABSOLUTELY not going to work, Eleanor thought. It had been another late night at the office. Max didn't seem to mind. He just had dinner, some delicious chicken casserole, waiting for her when she got home. Then after dinner, as they sat and watched TV, he picked up her feet and put them in his lap, rubbing every ounce of tightness away.

It was glorious. It was almost better than an orgasm.

And that's when she knew that if things stayed this way, if he kept being so kind and caring and considerate, then she had no hope of not falling in love with him again.

Of course, there was a case to be made that she'd never fallen out of love with him.

But she didn't want to go there. It was too much, and this space he'd created for them was a very safe place. They didn't talk about divorce or staying married. They didn't talk about their relationship or the future. They were just allowed to be. She liked that.

"Man, you are tight," he murmured, and she wished he hadn't sounded so sexy saying it. He was pressing his thumb into her arch, and she wanted to groan.

"Heels," she told him. "It's a love-hate relationship."

"Hmm. I also think it's stress. Now that we've been doing this living-together thing for a few days, I notice you don't talk much about the job. Is that because you don't want to or because you think I won't care?"

Eleanor considered that and shrugged. "It's not that I think you wouldn't care. I don't know. I guess Head to Toe has been so much my own thing for so long, I don't think about talking about it. And maybe there is a little more stress now. My natural inclination is to bury that so I can sleep at night."

"Is it the expansion?"

Eleanor shook her head. She hadn't told Max about Daniel's threats, mostly because she didn't know how he would react. The old Max would have been furious and threatening and would have offered to punch the guy out.

Nothing that would help the situation.

But this was the new Max. The more serious and sober, take-nothing-in-life-for-granted Max.

Who excelled at foot rubbing.

She had no idea how he might react. But did she have much to lose by telling him?

"You remember Daniel? From the engagement party?"

"I do."

"Well, our relationship, for lack of a better word, started as a series of business meetings. He's an investor and very much wants to invest in Head to Toe."

"But you don't want that."

"Maybe I'm too much of a control freak. I don't know. Or maybe because it was the only thing that kept me going…after. Besides, if I was going to take on a partner I would want that person to be Selena. She's earned it. All I know is that it's mine, and I didn't want to let it go. So I said no."

"Okay. Then what's the problem?"

"He's not taking no for an answer. He seems to be over whatever minor crush he had for me, now he just wants the company. Half of it."

Eleanor watched Max's face. His jaw tightened, but he seemed to be taking the news in stride.

"Yes, but you can still say no."

"He's implied that doing so would not be in my best interest."

Now she saw it. Real anger. Max stopped rubbing her feet. "Did he threaten you?"

"Yes, but listen, this is my problem to solve, okay? With the expansion, we're a little overextended, so there is the possibility he could cause some problems, but it's a business situation. Not a personal thing. You can't rush in and try to save the day."

"Let me at least help," Max insisted.

Eleanor reached out to pat his arm. "I know you want to, and I know you hate the idea of this guy hurting my company in any way, but you have to let me do this on my own. You have to respect that this is my area of expertise."

"I know, but you're not alone anymore, Nor. You don't have to handle everything on your own. I can help. I have money…"

She leaned into him and kissed his cheek. "Thank you for offering. And thank you for listening. But really, you have to let me do this myself. Owners of major companies figure this stuff out all the time. If I want to play with the big boys, then I have to learn how to handle situations like this that come up."

"Do you know how hard this is for me?"

Eleanor smiled. Yes, she did. Max was a man who wanted to fight battles, not sit on the sideline. It's why he'd always been so passionate about his work. It was a quality she'd loved about him.

"I know. You're actually being calmer than I thought you might be."

"I want to punch this guy in the face," he said tightly.

"Yes, but you won't. Ugh. I'm actually dreading seeing him again."

"Where? When?"

"There is a charity event we've both been invited to next week. He'll be there with his new girl of the month, no doubt. Which I couldn't care less about. Trust me when I tell you, I harbor nothing but ill will toward the man. But there had been speculation about us romantically. It's going to be awkward, and I really wasn't at my best the last time I saw him. I'm not looking forward to a repeat."

Max smiled wide enough that she could see his teeth, which probably wasn't a good thing.

"Then why don't you bring your new man of the month? I'll rent a tux, and then you won't have to do this thing alone."

Eleanor considered the idea. Having Max at her side, at her back. It wasn't the worst plan. She nodded. "You know that might actually work."

"Perfect. It's a date."

"It's an outing," she corrected him.

"I'll buy you a corsage," he said, wiggling his eyebrows.

"It's not a prom."

"Will there be dancing?"

"Yes."

"So it will be like a prom. We'll get gussied up, dance to nice music, and if this Daniel guy says one thing to you I don't like, then I get to push his face in the punch bowl."

Eleanor groaned. She could see the headlines. Dead Husband Back to Life Shoves Ex into Punch.

"Please tell me you won't do that."

Max shrugged. "I think you're better off hoping there is no punch."

ELEANOR SMOOTHED OUT her dress and took a deep breath. The party was a crush, which she imagined was a good thing for the charity. Denver's up-and-coming business owners along with some local sport celebrities were in attendance.

Max had excused himself to check their coats, and the loss of him felt a little jarring. It was like she'd gotten used to him in the past week always being there for her. Like having lost a vital body part, only to have it back again.

Like she was suddenly capable of doing more because she had Max.

That feeling was reinforced when he returned to her side. He was holding two flutes of champagne.

"Uh, forget something?" she asked him.

He drank a sip out of one, then handed it to her. "Just for show. You've got someone here who wants your company. He sees me at your side, and you're not drinking, it could lead to speculation. You want to avoid that."

"Good point," she said. And there it was. Max having her back. When always their roles had been reversed. She'd gone with him to the faculty parties. She'd filled him in on the names of the professors' wives and husbands. She'd been his rock.

Now he was hers.

"You know you've been really nice to me..."

He smiled. In that way he did that lit up his whole face. She wanted to reach out and touch that smile. Run her thumb along his bottom lip.

"I hate to let you in on the secret, but that's kind of my plan."

"Oh, there is a plan?"

"Yep. Step one—remind you that I'm a nice person."

"I think we can say that's been accomplished," she said.

"Step two—wow you with my cooking."

She chuckled. "You are surprisingly fairly competent in that department."

"Step three—seduce you."

Eleanor sucked in her breath, and her stomach dropped. Immediately she could feel a pulse between her legs. "Max..."

"Don't worry," he said, clearly retreating. "That's not until step three. You've got time to build up your defenses. Tonight all I want to do is dance with you."

Except with each passing hour she spent

with him building up her defenses was getting harder to do. The reason she'd pushed for the divorce in the first place was to prevent herself from falling into the Max trap.

She'd changed her mind about them because a divorce decree hadn't seemed to work on changing her feelings, and now that she was pregnant, they were connected anyway. So the question was what if she stopped fighting it? What if she stopped trying to defend her heart against him and just let herself fall?

Falling was scary.

Distracted, she lifted the glass to her lips without even realizing what she was doing. Fortunately the smell of champagne was off-putting enough to stop her.

"Eleanor! How nice to see you."

Max and Eleanor turned at the sound of the man's voice behind them. Daniel looked elegant in a white tux and bow tie.

"And of course… Dead Max. How nice to see you again, too."

"You'll forgive me if I don't believe that," Max said tightly.

Daniel smiled, but it didn't reach his eyes. The woman on his arm said nothing, and Daniel didn't bother to introduce her which Eleanor thought was rude. She wasn't used to rude Daniel. She'd always thought of him as so polite and charming.

Then again, the man wanted to steal her company. Not exactly a polite thing to do.

"Daniel," she said smoothly. "I hope you're well."

"Tolerable. Maybe a little bit of a heartache."

Eleanor didn't quite know what to say to that. And given that he was here with another woman, she couldn't imagine she'd left too much of an impression on him.

"So I hear you like to go around taking things that don't belong to you," Max said as he took a sip of his champagne. Eleanor put her hand on his arm. She wanted his support. She didn't need someone to fight her battles.

Daniel's smile faltered. "I'm a businessman. It's what I do. If Eleanor can't keep up with the game, then that's on her."

"People like you make me sick," Max snarled.

Sensing a punch-dunking in her near future, Eleanor stepped in front of him. She simply lifted her chin and looked at Daniel directly. "You're right, Daniel. It's on me to defend my company from the sharks that are out there. Do your worst, if you must. But I'm keeping Head to Toe. All of it."

"We'll see," he said. Then he dipped his chin and escorted the nameless blonde at his side into the crowd.

"Do your worst," Max repeated. "That sounded ballsy."

"Did it?" Eleanor hoped so, because she sure as heck had no clue what Daniel's worst was. "I wanted him to see me, know that I wasn't going to back down. But I really don't want to be here anymore. Do you think I've done my duty for the evening?"

Max took the glass from her hand and set it with his on a table. "Once around the room, with a big smile on your face, and a dance, because you promised me. And I want a chance to hold you in my arms. Then we can leave."

Another piece of sound advice. No problem here, her smile said. *Look at how I've got all my shit together. Nope, not falling apart on the inside while I deal with a husband back from the dead, an unexpected pregnancy and business shark out for my company.*

After a few hellos and some rounds of small talk, she felt like her face was going to crack.

But through it all Max was there. At her side. She tried not to think about how comforting it felt to have his hand on the small of her back. She tried not to think about how it felt beyond the comfort of letting her know he was close.

She'd always been very sensitive there. He knew that.

So when he pulled her onto the dance floor to sway with her to the sounds of the band and his thumb rubbed her casually through the silk of her dress, she couldn't help but shiver. He had to have felt it.

"Just a little longer," he said, pulling her closer into his arms. "You feel so good here. I had forgotten how much I loved to dance with you."

"Max," she said as if to chastise him, but in the end, she couldn't. She simply pressed her cheek against his and let him lead them around the dance floor. It was nice, but her feet were starting to hurt, and really, she didn't know how much longer she could keep a smile on her face.

He must have sensed she was at her limit because the next thing she knew he was leading her out of the hotel ballroom, tucking her into her coat and getting the valet to retrieve the car.

On the ride home, she was mostly quiet. There was a tension between them. She could feel it. It had been there since he laid out his three-step plan. What Max wanted had never been in doubt. He wanted her back, as his wife. In every way that meant.

They pulled up at her place and parked the car.

"All things considered, not a bad first date," he said.

"It wasn't a date. It was an event."

"You're wearing perfume. I'm wearing a tie. We danced…it was a date."

They made it to her front door as she pulled the keys out of her purse.

"I fake-smiled for most of the night…that can't be a good thing for a date."

He moved toward her, and this time she didn't back away.

"Yes, but when you real-smiled, it was at me. And it's the most beautiful thing in the world. I would like to kiss you now."

"You would?" she asked, nearly breathless.

"Well, if it was a date, then I suppose one kiss wouldn't hurt."

He leaned into her, and she could smell him first, the hint of his aftershave, or just his natural scent. To her, Max always smelled a little like the ocean. Then she was in his arms, and he was kissing her, and she didn't think about anything other than how good this felt. How right they always were together.

His finger stroked her chin, his hands dipped into her hair, and she had this thought that maybe they could stand here forever, doing their first-date kiss.

Until the door of her condo opened.

"Eleanor! Max!"

They broke away from the kiss to see a shocked and red-faced Allie.

"Allie, what are you doing here?"

"What am I doing here? Hello! What is he doing here? You divorced him, remember? Then you ran to my place to hide."

"You did?" Max asked Eleanor.

"She was completely freaked out and was afraid you were going to come after her. I think because she knew she was weak and would have caved."

"Allie!" Eleanor snapped at her sister.

"What? It's true. Which means he must not have given up because you were doing a whole lot of caving there. Kissing, caving. Same thing."

Eleanor took a breath for patience. "Allie, what are you doing here?"

That's when her sister promptly burst into tears. "The wedding's off," she cried through heavy sobs.

Max flinched, clearly unprepared to handle a despondent Allie.

"Can you make hot chocolate?" Eleanor asked him even as she was pulling Allie against her side.

"With whipped cream!" Allie shouted.

Max nodded. "I'm a man on a mission. You two go do your thing."

AN HOUR LATER, Allie sat on the couch sipping her hot chocolate. Max had run to the closest grocery store and gathered up the ingredients, including fresh whipping cream. Because if you were going to be consoled by whipped cream, only fresh would do.

Eleanor had changed out of her elegant gown into a tank top and pajama bottoms, her dark hair piled on top of her head. Allie thought it was a testament to how beautiful Eleanor was that she could go from a fancy dress and heels to pajamas and still pull off classy.

They were sitting on her couch while Max was still cleaning up in the kitchen.

"Are you going to tell me why he's here?" Allie asked her.

"Your story first. Why did you call off the wedding?"

"Because Mike and I just weren't meant to be. It's been obvious this entire time. All we do is fight about the wedding. This time it was over my hair and how I was going to wear it, and finally I said, I'm done. Who wants to spend their life in that kind of situation?"

Eleanor nodded, which really wasn't what Allie expected.

"You fought over your hair?" Eleanor said as she sipped her cocoa. "I didn't imagine Mike would be the kind of guy who had such a strong opinion about hair. Did he want you to wear it up? Or did you?"

Allie scowled at her sister. "You know that's not what it was about."

"I do, I'm just waiting for you to get there."

"Yes. Mom had an opinion. She has those. Lots of those. That's never going to stop. She thought I should wear it up, and I was considering her advice. That's all."

"And Mike was upset by that because…"

"I said I was going to wear it down, and he was glad because…because he said when I walked down the aisle he wanted to see me. Not someone who looked like me who he didn't know."

"Enter mother…and he's upset you're listening to her instead of doing what you want."

"I'm trying to make both of them happy!" Allie wailed. Why couldn't anyone understand that? It wasn't a bad thing. To make sure her mother, who loved her, was part of the experience. Taking advice when she offered it. Making her part of the process. Something she didn't get to have with Eleanor's wedding.

"Honey, that's the problem. You're trying to make *them* happy. Where do you fit in this? It's your wedding. Your day. You should be trying to make *you* happy."

Allie snorted. "That's my point. Any fun in this went out the window. It's all stress and work and compromise and fighting. There's no way this could actually work out between us."

"Sounds a lot like marriage," Max said, coming into the living room.

"No help from the peanut gallery, please," Eleanor said, glaring at him.

"Got it. Clearly, this is meant to be a man-free zone right now. I'll just head to bed."

"Good night."

Allie watched Max head upstairs. "Okay, can we pivot back to you now? How did you go from divorcing Max to living with him again? But wait a minute, I saw stuff in the guest bedroom. That doesn't make any sense."

"We're not *living* living together. We're... he's...well, don't be mad. I was going to tell you and Mom. I've just been... I don't know, maybe part of me still can't believe it..."

"Eleanor! Spit it out. You're scaring me here."

"I'm pregnant."

Allie's eyes grew wide as the word penetrated her brain. "A baby?"

Eleanor's small, quiet smile said exactly how she felt about that, too. She nodded.

"And Max..."

"Is the father."

Allie laughed, which felt good actually, because while leaving home to come here, she never thought she would be happy again. "He didn't waste any time in that cabin."

Eleanor blushed, but didn't speak about it. "Anyway, when I told him, he offered to stay with me and help out."

"So tonight outside your front door…that was him helping you?"

"Don't be dense, Allie. Obviously, there are feelings there, but I'm still…well, I don't know what I am. Not ready to be Max Harper's wife as if the past hadn't happened. That's all I know right now. It's all I can handle."

"The past is always going to be there, Eleanor. You can't undo what happened. You just have to figure out if you can move forward despite it."

Eleanor raised her eyebrow in that way she did when she was trying to be superior. Allie wanted to tell her how much she looked like Mom when she did that, but Eleanor always freaked out when anyone told her how much like their mother she was.

"I thought you came here to get advice, not to give it."

"I came here to run away like you did. I thought it would feel better."

Eleanor shook her head. "It doesn't. It just feels a lot like running away. You know you can't break up with Mike. You two love each other too much. You call things off and you're both bound to roam the earth as these sad, pathetic, lonely creatures silently longing for each other until your ultimate deaths."

"That's swell advice."

Eleanor shrugged and sipped her hot chocolate. "You know I'm right. This isn't about hair or stupid wedding stuff or even Mom. This is about Mike wanting you to stick up for yourself. And if you really are just taking Mom's opinions to heart because you know it makes her happy and not because you feel you have to, then Mike needs to understand that, too. It's okay to be the good daughter. Marilyn should at least have one."

Allie smirked. "Please, you are about to give Marilyn a grandchild. You're so going to be the number-one daughter. Now she might put a preference in for the sex of that child..."

Eleanor rubbed her belly. "Sorry. No requests."

"Mike will be worried about me," Allie sighed. "He won't like that I was driving while crying my eyes out."

"Then you better call him and tell him you made it here safely. Then you can tell him you don't want to be a sad zombie roaming the earth pining for him."

Allie nodded. "Yeah."

Max came down the stairs. "Not interrupting, but, Allie, I wanted to let you know I changed the sheets on the guest bed. The room is yours for the night."

"Thanks, Max."

"Uh, where are you going to sleep?" Eleanor asked him.

"With you," he said, smiling. "Surely, you can handle sleeping beside me for one night, can't you?"

Allie snorted. "Looks like you just went from living together to *living* living together."

"As my younger sister I still have the right to hit you," Eleanor muttered.

"You can't tussle with me," Allie reminded her. "Not in your fragile condition."

Then she watched as Eleanor rubbed her

hand over her belly as if she still couldn't believe something was in there.

"You're going to be a great mom."

"A mom," Eleanor whispered reverently. "It's crazy. I went from being a widow and a boss to a wife again and a soon-to-be mother in a very short amount of time."

Allie nudged her sister's shoulder. "I'm so happy for you. It's nice to see you smile again and know that you're really feeling it."

Eleanor nodded.

"Of course, you know you need to tell Mom."

"Yep."

Allie laughed. "You'll see. You'll like being the one making her happy."

CHAPTER EIGHTEEN

MAX WATCHED HIS wife as she puttered about her bedroom. She was rubbing lotion up and down her arms, and he was trying not to get turned on by it and failing. She was stalling, he knew, and he thought it was rather adorable. She was skittish about sleeping with him again.

The last time they did this, they woke up kissing, which would have led to more if she hadn't panicked. After a week of living together, a week of being there for her, he could sense he was wearing her down.

Not the most romantic of thoughts for a man to have about wooing his wife, but Max was desperate.

Eventually, she pulled down the covers and crawled into bed. She smelled of lavender and Nor, and Max thought he'd never been so happy.

"You know, Nor, I never thought you were

the kind of girl who slept with a guy on the first date."

For that, he was awarded a small decorative pillow to the face.

He laughed, tucked the pillow behind his head, then reached over to turn off the light.

Turning on his side, facing her back, he bent down and asked, "Can I hold you? Just hold you. I promise. No funny business."

He waited a beat, then the subtle nod of her head gave him all the encouragement he needed. He pressed himself against her and brought his hand around her waist.

"Can I hold the baby, too?"

Again, another nod. Max rested his hand over her lower belly. He told himself he could feel the smallest change in her body, but he knew he was reaching. Looking for something that wasn't visible yet. He just wanted it to be.

"I thought about this...on the life raft."

Her body stiffened, but he immediately started making soothing sweeps over her belly.

"I thought about how you wanted to talk about getting pregnant, and I said we could put it off. Like life is infinite. Like it's all under our control and we can have anything we want, whenever we want it. All of it on our time lines. I was such a cocky asshole."

"You were passionate. You thought you could change the world. You wanted to do that first."

He had thought he could change the world. He could fix the planet and change people's minds and their habits.

When the whole time this world, the one in his arms, was right there in front of him. He pulled her against him, tighter. "I'm never going to leave you, Nor. You might decide to kick me out and divorce my ass, but if you have the smallest doubt that I might go back to how it was, know this… I get it now. I had everything. I have another chance at everything and more, and I'm never going to blow that chance again."

She didn't say anything, and, for a moment, he wondered if she'd fallen asleep.

"I'm trying, Max," she whispered.

Trying, he thought, was a million miles from divorce papers. Trying was hope.

The words were on his tongue. He wanted to tell her he loved her again. That he'd never stopped, not for one day, even when he'd come back from his assignment to find that she'd left him.

But if he was coming to understand something about this new version of his wife, it was that she was cautious and thoughtful. The last time he'd said it, he'd spooked her.

He needed to recognize what he'd done to her, the pain he'd caused her, and live with the consequences. Even as he worked on overcoming it. After all, he was trying, too.

Trying. He couldn't remember a time when a single word had made him so happy.

THE FIRST THING he thought about when he woke up the next morning was Nor. In some ways it felt like the dreams he used to have when he was stuck on the island in pain. Always in pain.

He would go to that place in his head where it was just them, nuzzled in their bed, neither one ready to start the day. A sense of contentment that he'd had the first time he'd slept with her overnight when they had been dating.

This was like that. He was on his side, she was wrapped around his back, her thigh on top of his and her hand was moving around his waist, dipping into the elastic on his pajama bottoms…as if she was going to…going to…

"Oh, yes," he hissed as her hand found his hard, aching cock. She stroked him with long, slow tugs and groaned.

"They say that pregnant women can be hormonal, which can result in…" She trailed off because he knew she wasn't willing to admit that she was horny as hell.

"Needing my dick?"

"Something like that."

Max rolled over, her hand leaving his erection which made him sad. "I would hate to leave you in such a frustrated state." Even as he said it, he pressed his cock against her center, and she tilted her head back and moaned.

"Shhhh, we have to be quiet," he reminded her. "Allie's just across the hall."

"Nope. She left about an hour ago. I heard her leave."

"Oh. Then we can be as loud as we want because I think I would like to make you scream my name."

She shook her head against the pillow. "I do have neighbors."

"Don't care," Max said even as he slithered

his way down her body. He stopped and pulled the straps of her tank top down her arms, freeing her breasts from their confines.

Her nipples were already hard, and, as he took them into his mouth, Max enjoyed the feel of her squirming beneath him. He used to have fantasies about tying her arms behind her back and teasing and playing with her nipples for hours until she was a writhing case of need. However, this morning didn't feel like the time for teasing. This was about satisfaction.

Max moved down a little farther and pulled her bottoms down over her hips.

"Max," she said. For whatever reason, Nor had always been shy about oral sex. Like she was asking too much from him. Receiving too much pleasure without having to do enough of the work.

It always used to take some coaxing with her, just as it did this morning.

"Please, Nor. It's been so long. I need this. I need to taste you again."

And he did need it. The taste of her, the smell of her, the sounds he knew he could wring from her.

Max was fighting for their marriage, and

each and every day with her was its own battle. Whether he could help her get through an awkward night with a business foe, or rub her feet or give her intense pleasure, all of that was going to make a case. For a future for them.

A family.

He ran his fingers through her slick heat and slowly and carefully opened her up to his touch. Then he pulled the pajamas off her and tossed them out of his way, sinking down between her legs. Her eyes were closed. Her arm, thrown over them as if she needed the extra protection of not watching.

Which was the polar opposite of him. There was nothing he loved more than watching Nor go down on him. Seeing his cock in her mouth and feeling it at the same time was nothing short of spectacular.

Except he needed to remove that mental image if he was going to focus on her and not his raging need to be inside of her. He rubbed his tongue along her clit and listened as she sighed. Like she couldn't help but make the breathy sounds. He tormented her and teased her. Coming close but never doing enough to get her where she needed because when that happened he wanted to be inside her.

He wanted to be inside his wife.

"Max!"

Max lifted his head and pushed his own bottoms down over his ass. He didn't hesitate, but instead thrust deep inside her slick heat. He could feel her go over the edge.

Home. Home. Home. The word just kept running over and over again.

Then he was exploding with her, and his world became the sound of his name on his wife's lips.

ALLIE PARKED THE car behind the house and noticed that Mike's truck was there. She cringed. She'd been hoping for a little bit of a reprieve, but it didn't look like she would get it.

She got out of the car and made her way through the back door of the house, which opened into the kitchen. Mike was sitting at the kitchen table with a newspaper—because he still liked the feel of an actual newspaper— and a cup of coffee.

He turned to her as the door opened but didn't say anything.

"Coffee still warm?" she asked as a way of a greeting.

"Should be," he said in a way of an answer.

Allie decided fighting sucked. Especially when she was the person in the wrong. She poured herself a cup and made her way to sit at the table with him.

"I'm sorry," she said. It helped that there were words a person could immediately go to in this situation.

"Sorry for what?" Mike asked her.

"For all of it. For getting all worked up and breaking things off. For running to Eleanor."

"I was worried," he grunted still reading his newspaper. "You were crying pretty hard when you left."

"I'm sorry for that, too," Allie said. "You know I don't want that. For us to be over."

"Do I?"

"Mike," Allie sighed sadly. "Please don't make this any harder on me. I said I was sorry."

He shook his head. "I'm not trying to make this hard on you, Allie. I love you. I just don't want to keep doing this."

"I agree with that. I hate fighting with you over every little thing."

"We're not fighting over every little thing. We're fighting about one thing, and we're not going to stop until you figure your shit out. This is bigger than your mother being pushy."

That hurt. As if she alone was the cause of all their problems lately. "I don't consider my mother *shit*," she grumbled.

He growled. "That's not what I meant and you know it."

He ran his hand through his hair in frustration, and Allie had this sudden urge to run her own fingers through it. Straighten it out. She hated that she was making him feel this way.

"Marilyn is Marilyn," Mike said. "I get that. I have told you that before. Hell, I even like the woman despite how pushy she can be. However, what I'm not going to do is spend my life watching you fall over yourself to please that woman at the expense of your happiness. Because that's the thing, Allie. It doesn't end there. The next thing I know, you'll be doing the same with me. Every decision we make will be about what I want. And the whole time I'll be wondering are you doing what you're doing because you want it, too, or just because

I want it. I want a woman who is stronger than that."

That hurt, too.

"I'm not Eleanor!" Allie screeched. "Okay? I didn't go off to college and pay for it on my own. I didn't elope with the guy I wanted to marry because I didn't want to listen to my mother. I didn't start my own zillion-dollar company. I'm not strong like her. I thought you knew that."

Mike was staring at her hard. "You think this is about Eleanor?"

No. It wasn't as if she thought for a minute Mike had a thing for her sister. She just felt like he was asking her to be someone she wasn't. When all this time she thought he loved her for who she was.

"What if I can't be that woman you say you want?"

"Allie, you are the woman I want. All I'm asking you to do is to be you. Because I know it's how you are. I know you like to make people happy. Hell, it's the first thing I fell in love with…your generosity. But I told you before, I know how this works. If you're doing everything you can to make me happy, without thinking about yourself, you'll come to resent me, too. Knowing you might feel that way about me would break me."

"I could never..." Could she? Resent always trying to make Mike happy.

He rose from the table and took his cup to the sink. "I need to head into town for some supplies. You need anything?"

"I guess a spine."

He huffed out a laugh. "No, I'm pretty sure you've got one of those. But I sure would like to see you use it now and again."

She sat there and sipped her coffee and thought about what he said.

What did she want?

Mike. That was an easy answer. To be married to him. Another easy answer. To have the kind of love that lasted like Eleanor and Max's. To make her mother happy, because that wasn't wrong to want to do that.

To make herself happy. Because that wasn't wrong to want to do that, either.

"I know what I don't want and that's some stupid, big wedding," she muttered to the empty room. "If I could just find a way to have it be me and Mike and make Mom happy."

Unfortunately the magic answer didn't immediately come.

ELEANOR STARED AT the phone. It was Saturday, and Max had gone out to run some errands. Most Saturdays Eleanor would spend at the office, but after being thoroughly made love to this morning, followed by a shower in which Max made it his personal responsibility to wash every inch of her, she just had no motivation to work. And every motivation to sit on her couch with her feet up.

The only task she'd assigned herself was calling her mother. It was a tough call to make. On the one hand, Allie was probably right and her mother might be thrilled. On the other hand, Eleanor knew her mother was not Max's biggest fan.

Eleanor found her mother's number in her favorites list and hit the button. A few seconds later, her mother picked up.

"Hi, Mom."

"What's wrong?"

Eleanor shook her head. "Why do you assume I only ever call you when something is wrong?"

There was a pause. "Because you call me once a week on Sunday. If you're calling me on a Saturday, something is wrong."

"Nothing is wrong. Exactly. I just have news."

"Yes?"

Eleanor could practically see her mother's raised eyebrow. There was no help for it. It was like ripping off a bandage.

"I'm pregnant."

Another pause, only this time longer.

"Mom, did you hear me?"

"Of course I heard you!" her mother screeched. "I'm assuming Max is the father."

"The trip to the cabin," Eleanor said weakly.

"What about the divorce? Is there a way to stop it? Will you have to be remarried?"

"I haven't really thought about that..."

"How could you not think of it? He's the father of your child. You need to be married to him."

Eleanor thought about explaining to her mother that it was the twenty-first century and it was not considered that unusual anymore for a woman to have a baby on her own. She didn't say that, of course, mostly because it would upset her, and the truth was, she wanted to be married to Max.

Or stay married to Max.

Or get married to Max.

It was confusing as hell, but the net result of that was she was willing to admit to herself that she wanted Max.

"We'll work it out," Eleanor finally said.

"And what happens when he leaves again? What then?"

Eleanor felt the sinking pit in her stomach. That fear that her mother was right and Max wasn't capable of changing who he was. Of needing to continue his research and the impact of climate change so that, ultimately, he might save the world.

Then she remembered what he'd said to her last night. Holding her and their baby.

"He's not going to leave again," Eleanor said softly as if she was trying the words out and seeing how they sounded. She wasn't exactly sure if she believed them.

"You have no idea if that's true or not."

"No, Mom. I think I do know. I don't think he's going to leave me again."

"So you two are together now?"

Were they? She knew Max was all in. He'd pretty much proclaimed that from the start. She, however, felt as if she was keeping one foot outside the door. Ready to run at the first sign of emotional pain.

That wasn't going to work long-term. No relationship could stand that kind of ambiguity. Beyond that, Max deserved better. He deserved someone who was willing to commit to him fully.

"It's complicated," Eleanor said, even though that sounded lame to her ears.

"Huh. Complicated. You know what's not complicated...a baby. How are you planning to raise this child?"

Eleanor didn't want to think about that because it meant thinking about the future. And right now, the future was too scary.

"We're working that out, too."

"Hmm. And what about that company of yours?"

Eleanor cringed. Her mother referred to her

company as if it was an ex-convict boyfriend. "What about it?"

"Well, you're not going to be able to dedicate as much time as you have to it and raise a baby. It's simply not possible."

"No, not without help, of course."

"Babies need their mothers."

"And their fathers. Stop being so old school, Mom."

"I'm old school, because I'm old. Well, there is only one answer. If you're going to insist on raising this child on your own and still run your company, I'll have to come live with you."

And Eleanor thought that was as good a reason as any to tell Max she was all in. She smiled. "Mom, we're not there yet. I told you. Max and I are working it out."

"Well, work it out faster. I'm not letting my first grandchild be raised by some strange nanny you hire just so you can keep your company. My first grandchild…"

Her mother broke off for a moment. Eleanor held the phone closer to her ear. Was that…? Was it possible? Was her mother crying?

"Mom, are you crying?"

"Tears of joy. I'm going to be a grandmother finally. I think I'm allowed."

Eleanor smiled. Allie was right. It did feel good to be the one making her mother happy for once.

"Of course this means we're going to have to rethink your maid-of-honor dress. My goodness, you'll be almost ready to pop on the day of the wedding. Do you know how hard it is going to be to find something chic and elegant in a maternity gown?"

"Sorry, Mom, but I'm sure you'll come up with something."

"You'll let me pick out the dress?"

Eleanor smiled. Who knew it really wasn't all that difficult to make her mother happy. "I get final approval."

"It's a deal. And, Eleanor...I want you to know I am happy. I want this thing between you and Max to work. I do. I just..."

She had trust issues. It happened to a woman when she was burned in a marriage.

"I know, Mom. You'll see. I think it will all work out. Goodbye."

"Goodbye."

Eleanor ended the call and thought about what it would mean for it to all work out and knew that the answer was with her.

But that, she decided, was a problem for another day.

CHAPTER NINETEEN

MAX KNOCKED LIGHTLY on the outside of the office door. Selena and Nor were huddled over some spreadsheets, and both popped their heads up. He held up the bag of to-go food, and Nor waved him inside.

"You are a lifesaver," Selena said, rushing toward him to take the bag.

It was after nine at night. Max had texted Eleanor for an update on when she would be home and she'd texted back TROUBLE.

He figured that meant food, so he brought the food to them.

"You both must be starving."

"Not me," Nor said. "I've been nibbling on saltines all day. This kid has decided it doesn't like real food."

Selena lifted a burger and a sleeve of fries out of the bag, and Max watched Nor's face go sheet white.

She covered her mouth and practically ran from the office.

"And she's off!" Selena said. "Don't worry. She does that about three times a day, and she always comes back feeling better. She'll be able to eat something then, too."

Max let out a sigh of relief. He hated seeing her sick, but at the same time, he'd read that morning sickness was a good sign for the pregnancy.

They were just about at the sixteen-week mark, and for the first time, he could see Nor's stomach starting to round out. It was becoming more real every day. So was their marriage.

After Allie left, Max didn't bother moving his stuff back into the guest room. That first night, he'd just told Nor he was going to bed and climbed into her bed. She'd said nothing, and when she got in and he spooned himself around her, she'd relaxed against him.

From that point on, they had slept together every night. And the sex, it was like they didn't talk about what it meant. Like he was simply servicing his wife's hormonal needs. Something he was happy to do. Much like rubbing her feet.

Except he knew it went way deeper than that. They were bonding again, connecting down to their toes. Nor just wasn't ready to talk about that yet.

"She said there was trouble."

"We have a cash-flow problem. One of our servers went down unexpectedly last week, which stopped orders for two days, which means our sales weren't as projected. Now we have to pay our contractors and—"

"You don't have any money," Max said, figuring out the situation quickly.

"Don't say that!" Nor scolded him as she came into the office. Her color had returned, and he could smell the hint of mint toothpaste. "At least not out loud."

Selena rolled her eyes. "With pregnancy has come paranoia. She's convinced that Daniel has planted bugs in the office."

"I didn't say that. Just that we have to be careful. This is exactly the kind of trip-up he's waiting for. If we can't pay the contractors and we lose those contracts, then we're done. I'll have no option but to take his offer."

"I have money," Max announced.

"We'll take it," Selena said clapping.

"Selena! Max, I'm not taking your money."

"Why not?"

"Because this is my problem, and I'll solve it."

Max rocked back on his heels. "Selena… could you give us a minute?"

Selena looked to him, then at Eleanor. "Sure."

She took her burger and her phone and shut the office door behind her.

"Max, I don't really have time to argue over this."

"Tough."

Her eyebrows went up, but he wasn't backing down. "I want to know why you won't take my money. I haven't even told you how much of it there is."

"I told you…"

"That it's your problem. Yeah, I got that. When is it going to be *our* problem? We've been living together for weeks. Sleeping together for weeks. Having sex for weeks. Are we in a marriage or are we not?" Max snapped.

"I…we… I mean, it's been good… I know that."

He could see he was upsetting her, but, damn

it, he was angry. "Because I don't know what to do anymore, Nor. I don't know how to prove, once and for all, that I'm in this marriage for real. Every day is like this exquisite torture wondering if today is the day I'll know. I'll know for sure that you see a future with me."

"You think taking your money means I'm ready to commit to you?"

"No, taking my money would tell me you already had committed. Which obviously, you haven't. I'll leave you to *your* problem, but can you try not to work too much later? You are pregnant. You need some damn sleep."

Max didn't wait for a response. He left the office and kept moving until he reached his car. He stopped and took a breath. Fighting with his pregnant sort of wife was probably not the solution to the problem.

And worse was the fact that she was in actual trouble and wasn't letting him help. There had to be a way. Then he realized there was.

He pulled out his phone and searched through his list of contacts. He'd added Selena to his list weeks ago. It made him feel better knowing she could reach out to him at any time if Nor had had problems with the baby.

Mostly Selena only texted him when she was dead on her feet tired and she wanted him to prod Nor into calling it a night.

It had actually worked a few times.

He hit her number and waited until she picked up. She was obviously still chewing a rather large bite of her hamburger.

"'Sup?"

"You guys need money. I have it. A lot of it. Money that Nor doesn't even know about. How do we find a way to get that to you?"

"Are you saying you want me to sneak behind my boss's back and arrange for a financial loan?"

"That's exactly what I'm saying. With the guarantee that if she's going to be furious with anyone, it's going to be me."

"Okay, I'm in. And, Max…for the record, I know it seems like she's holding back. I get why that would be frustrating, too. But…"

"But?"

"I didn't know her before you…went missing. I've only known her since. And the Eleanor I know is smart and strong and decisive… and sad. Or at least she was until several weeks ago. She's different now. I can see it. Weary, but...hopeful. I guess I'm saying, don't give up on her."

Suddenly all his anger was so much smoke. Now he had someone to confirm he was making Nor happy again. It felt amazing. "I won't."

"Good. Call me tomorrow and we'll talk about options."

"Thanks, Selena."

Max disconnected the call with a scowl. At least now he had a plan. He just had to convince Nor it was a good one.

ELEANOR TRIED TO pull her pants together and failed. It simply was not going to happen. Her days of wearing her normal business suits were over. Which sucked on a day when she wanted to look her most formidable.

Instead, she was going to have to go with leggings, boots and a tunic top. It wasn't as if she was concerned about Daniel knowing she was pregnant anymore. The reality was in less than five months or so there was going to be a baby. It was thoughts of that baby and what her mother had said that made her pick up the phone and schedule this meeting.

She'd thought about it all. The baby, Max,

what Daniel intended for Head to Toe. Maybe Daniel had been right and she just wasn't capable of playing in the big leagues. And if she wasn't able to do it now, what made her think she could do all that and be a mother?

And a wife.

Because when it came down to it, that's what she wanted to be. She wanted to be Max's wife. Not his half-wife, or his sort-of wife, which, he liked to joke about, but his wife, wife.

Which meant committing to their relationship and him. Which meant spending time together as a family.

Turning over half her company to Daniel meant turning over half the responsibility of running it, too. So maybe this was the best solution for everyone. Tell Daniel she was willing to take his money, let him worry about taking the company big league and focus on working on her marriage and being a new mom.

It was a solid plan. She knew that. She just wished it felt better. More like winning and less like losing.

Dressed, she made her way downstairs. Max was at the kitchen counter having a cup of coffee. He was also dressed for class, and it occurred to her how little they talked about his teaching.

Of course not, stupid. You're afraid to ask him about it and find out that he doesn't like it.

Which was really kind of horrible on her part and all indicative of the trust issues she still needed to work out with him.

She thought about the meeting she was headed to and realized she probably should have informed him of her decision. It was something he would want her to do, to share what was happening with her company, because it was a part of their life.

In the end, though, she felt like this needed to be her call alone. She'd built Head to Toe from the ground up. She'd done it first to prove to Max she was capable of being more than just his wife. Then she'd stayed at it because there was nothing else for her.

Now if she was going to end this journey, or maybe not end it, but hand part of it over, then that had to be her call, too.

"'Morning," Max said with a weary smile.

"My pants don't fit," Eleanor announced.

That made him smile even more.

"Oh, sure, you think it's a cute baby thing, but I'm down to leggings and tunic tops."

"Guess we're going to need to go shopping. I hear they make these things called maternity clothes."

Eleanor frowned, thinking about jeans that stretched. Then she remembered she'd given her mother carte blanche on the dress she would wear to Allie's wedding. A wedding that, as far as Eleanor knew, was still on, which meant Allie must be working things out with the Mike.

Not that Eleanor had any doubt. Mike and Allie loved each other, and as long as that was the case, the rest didn't matter.

Then it occurred to her how true that was.

"Max?"

He was pouring her orange juice and setting out her prenatal vitamins. That's what he did for her every morning, because if he didn't, she usually forgot. Because Max was thoughtful and caring and supportive and amazing.

And he told her he wasn't going to leave.

"Hmm?"

I love you.

The words were there. All she had to do was say them.

She imagined how happy he would be. Because he would know what those words meant. That she was finally ready to do this big and amazing thing with him. To fall in love…again. To believe that it could be true.

I love you.

Three simple words.

"You know I think you're amazing," she said instead.

He smiled, really smiled, at her, and she knew that his anger from the previous night was gone.

"Eleanor Gaffney Harper, you've made me the happiest man alive."

She beamed. It wasn't the big words. Not yet. But she was sure they would come. She just needed more time.

"I'm glad."

"Hey, Nor. You know I love you, right? Even when you make me angry."

She nodded. She felt loved. So much so that she had the courage to do this thing she needed to do.

"What time is your class over?" she asked him. "Maybe we can grab lunch today?"

"I'll be done by twelve, and that sounds great."

"Sounds great now. Just wait until the puking starts," she reminded him.

"I'll take my chances. Now go rule the world."

Her smile tightened. She should tell him, she thought. She should tell him what she was going to do because she didn't have to be alone anymore. But then he kissed the tip of her nose and was heading out the door with a "Goodbye and see you in a few hours."

Lunch, she thought. She would tell him at lunch. After it was done.

DANIEL'S OFFICE WAS every bit as impressive as she was sure he knew it to be. Surrounded by glass, beautiful mountain view. Spacious. Intimidating.

She sat in the chair across from his desk as he ended a phone call. His admin assistant had asked if she wanted any coffee or tea, which Eleanor had politely turned down.

Technically caffeine was against the rules, so she limited herself as much as she could.

She touched her belly and watched as Daniel's gaze drifted down. She doubted he could actually see her bump, the outfit she wore basically hid everything, but still it was something she didn't want to discuss with him.

This was business, not personal. Any guilt she felt over ending their fledging relationship when Max came back into her life was gone the minute Daniel told her he cared more about her company than he did about her.

Which was why she didn't want to discuss Max, her pregnancy or anything else that wasn't related to Head to Toe. This was going to be hard enough without the baggage.

"Yep. Got it. Got to go. My eleven o'clock is here. Okay. Thanks," Daniel said, finishing up. He clicked a button on his headset and took it off. Fancy, state-of-the-art, wireless Bluetooth. She wanted to tell him it left his hair messed up, but she didn't.

He smiled at her, and she had to force herself to smile back.

"Eleanor, I can't tell you how happy I am you called."

"Well, I have had a lot of time to think about your offer—"

"And of course, there was that technical glitch you had last week. Probably had a significant adverse effect on cash flow, I imagine."

Eleanor tensed. "Heard about that, huh?"

"Let's just say I have sources," he said smoothly.

"Does *sources* mean corporate spies?" she asked tightly.

He laughed. "Don't be ridiculous."

"Right, because ridiculous might be thinking about the timing of the technical glitch. And how, strangely, it happened now of all times."

"Naturally. That would be ridiculous."

Eleanor wanted to hurl something at his smug face, but the truth was she had to rise above it. She was here to make a deal. A sound deal that would both benefit her company and immediately resolve any cash-flow issues. She had to think more like a businesswoman and less like a pissed-off woman.

"You said you want half of Head to Toe—"

Except now, he was shaking his head. "No, Eleanor. I wanted half of Head to Toe. That was before you needed me."

She braced for whatever he was going to say next.

"Now I want sixty percent."

"Controlling interest," she said tightly.

"I prefer being the boss. Making the final call. You understand. With sixty percent control I can bring in who I want to manage things as I see fit."

Her company. This thing she'd built from the ground up. This thing that had defined her for the past almost three years. Now he didn't want to share it. He wanted to take control. Suddenly, she knew immediately that she didn't want to make this decision by herself.

She wanted to talk it over with Max. Get his input. Maybe see if he had another idea. What she didn't want to do was cower.

Instead, she stood to her full height.

"I see. You've changed the offer on the table," she said calmly. "Of course I'll need time to reconsider."

"Of course. But just know every day that you take to consider results in me wanting more. I want to be reasonable, Eleanor, but—"

"But you're a businessman."

"Yes."

"I'll have an answer for you shortly, then." She started to walk away.

"I hate to ask. These things can be so delicate…but should I be offering you congratulations of a personal nature?"

Sources, my ass. Everyone in the company knew she was pregnant. And so did Daniel.

She turned to him and smoothed the tunic over her baby bump, outlining the shape for him to clearly see. "Actually, yes."

"That seems to have happened rather quickly," he said. And that's when she knew this wasn't just business for him. No matter what he said. This was about Daniel losing and clearly, he didn't take it very well.

Eleanor beamed at him. "Let's just say Max is…very virile. Nice chatting with you, Daniel. I'll be sure to be in touch."

"Yes," he said tightly. "You do that. The clock is ticking. Tick, tock."

Douchebag. Eleanor, however, did not say that. She didn't want to give him the satisfaction.

THE DRIVE TO the campus was fairly easy, which was probably a good thing since she couldn't stop thinking about her meeting with Daniel.

All she wanted to do was see Max and tell him everything. And know that she wasn't alone.

Eleanor parked the car in front of the sciences building and let herself think about that for a moment.

She wasn't alone. It was the reality of having Max back in her life. It was strange to only see now how isolated she had been for the past few years. For a moment, she felt a pang of guilt. For her mother. Allie. She hadn't really been there for either of them. It had been so easy to say that was because of the company and the effort she'd put in to building it. But now she knew more of it had been a result of grief.

Grief and loss and missing Max.

Giddy with the idea that she could see him in a few minutes, she bounced out of her SUV and made her way inside the large brick building where she knew he was finishing up his class.

She had to ask a student coming down the hallway which classroom was his, but once she had that she was able to navigate the sea of students pouring out of the room.

It was a large classroom, one of those auditorium-type setups and, strangely, it filled her with pride. She'd forgotten how important

Max was in this particular area. The rock star of climate change research.

His work had been groundbreaking and eye-opening. Some might say lifesaving. It made sense that he would attract a large crowd to hear him share what he'd learned. The last students were leaving, and she could see Max behind a lectern talking to an older man with a thick bush of gray hair and an ill-fitting suit coat.

She knew that head of hair, the slump of the man's shoulders. Tom Hadly was the director of the research program that had sent Max, and her with him, to Norway. It had been Tom's fund-raising that drove Max out onto the ocean time and time again.

"We have a deal then?" Tom asked Max.

Eleanor felt her heart skip a beat. Tom sounded hopeful.

Then she looked at her sort-of husband, who smiled broadly and shook the older man's hand. "Absolutely."

He was leaving again. He said he wouldn't, but he'd just been offered something big, no doubt. Something bigger than before and the lure of fieldwork would be impossible to resist.

"You liar!" The words burst from her chest, and she covered her belly as if she could protect the child in her womb from knowing her father would abandon her.

"Eleanor, hello," Tom said, not understanding the sudden tension in the classroom. "Good to see you again. I was just catching up with Max…"

"You said you wouldn't leave, and you lied!" Eleanor said, looking at Max, not having any time for what Tom was saying.

She spun on her heel and started to climb the steps as fast as her feet would carry her.

"Nor! Wait, it's not what you think."

She didn't have to hear it. She didn't have to listen to whatever excuse he was going to offer. He would tell her how important the work was. He would tell her that his work was bigger than their marriage.

Bigger than their child?

That didn't seem right that he could believe that, but she knew. Tom and the deal and *absolutely*…she knew what that meant. She made her way out of the room and found a place where he couldn't follow her.

Ducking into the nearest ladies' room, she

listened as he shouted for her down the hall. Not seeing her, obviously, not knowing where she'd gone. She could hear him running, his shoes clicking against the linoleum floor. The unsteady gait of his run and she couldn't help but think it must be hurting his leg.

She waited until she was sure the hallway was clear, then made her way out a side exit. She found her car, got in and thought how it had only been a few minutes ago when she'd been so damn happy. So damn sure that everything between them was going to work out.

Slamming her hands against the steering wheel, she wanted to howl her rage at the world. Why wasn't she enough? Why weren't she and the baby enough for him?

Eleanor took a breath, then another. She needed to calm down if she was going to drive. She wouldn't put herself or her baby in danger. She thought about going to the condo, but that would be the first place he would go looking for her, and she truly didn't want to listen to his excuses.

She thought of going to her mother, but could only imagine what Marilyn's reaction would be.

Once a leaver, always a leaver.

Marilyn had never forgiven Eleanor's father for what he had done to her, but Eleanor had been so close to moving forward with Max. So close to putting the past really behind them and taking this miraculous second chance at love.

She'd almost done it this morning! Almost told him she loved him.

She started the car and left the college behind her. She couldn't go home, she couldn't go to her mother. She didn't want to put any more stress on Allie than what she was already going through with Mike and the wedding.

Alone. Alone again like she had been before. There was only one place she could think of where being alone and away from everyone might bring her some comfort. Making her way to the highway, she set her course for the mountains.

CHAPTER TWENTY

"Nor! You home?" Max could hear how silent the condo was. "Shit." He tried her phone again, but she wasn't picking up. He tried not to panic. Eventually she would have to see him again. Eventually they would have to talk, and he could explain that she had completely misunderstood the deal he'd made with Tom Hadly.

Max appreciated how it must have looked to her. Tom was the person behind all of his fieldwork assignments. She saw him shaking Tom's hand and just assumed that they had come to another agreement. But it couldn't be further from the truth.

Hell, the deal he'd made had been for Eleanor.

He picked up his phone and called Selena.

"Max, what's up?"

"Is Nor there with you?"

"No, she had her meeting with Daniel, and

then she was supposed to be having lunch with you."

"What meeting with Daniel?"

There was a beat of silence.

"Selena," Max pushed.

"She didn't tell you. Shit. She's going to kill me because she probably wanted to do this herself, but she was going to take the deal."

A rush of shock flooded him. That she hadn't told him. That she was even considering it. "No. She wouldn't give up her company."

"I think she kind of talked herself into thinking it would be a good idea. You know, with you and the baby coming..."

Max was angry then. "I didn't want her to do that. I was fixing things so he couldn't hold the threat over her head anymore. You knew that."

"She just told me this morning. I didn't know what to say about the money..."

Max rubbed a hand over his face. "It's not your fault. I shouldn't have put you in that position. Damn it."

"Should I be worried?" Selena asked him, and he could hear the fear in her voice. "Did she not meet you for lunch?"

"She saw me, but she...she mistook a conversation I was having. She thinks I was making plans to leave her, but I wasn't. I have to find her."

There was another beat of silence. "What can I do?"

"Call her, will you? Don't tell her I've been in touch with you. If she doesn't think you know anything, she might tell you where she's going."

"First, going behind her back with the money, and now this. You're seriously asking me to break the sisterhood code."

Max was desperate. "Please, Selena. I—I love her. I have to talk to her. She has to know the truth."

"Okay. I'll try. For her own good."

"Thanks."

Max ended the call and waited. Maybe she wouldn't pick up for Selena. Maybe she was off somewhere driving while distraught. Not paying attention. What if there was an accident? All because of some stupid misunderstanding.

A few minutes later, his phone rang.

"She says she needs to be alone," Selena said.

"Because she thinks I lied to her. She needs to understand the truth."

A deep sigh. "Okay. She's gone to the cabin."

Max closed his eyes with relief. "Thank you, Selena."

"You better fix this, Max. She sounded brokenhearted."

"Trust me. I am going to do everything I can to put that heart back together once and for all."

MAX ARRIVED AT the cabin just as the sun was setting. He parked the car and was again flooded with relief when he saw Nor's car already there. He pulled his duffel bag out of the car and made his way up the steps. The door wasn't locked, so he let himself in.

Eleanor was on the couch, not facing him. Her shoulders shaking. The sounds of her sobs masked the sound of him dropping his bag and closing the door behind him. Slowly so as not to startle her, he came into the room and walked around the edge of the couch until she looked up and gasped. A half sob stuck in her throat.

"Nor, I need you to listen to me."

"I don't want to. I don't want to hear you say it," she cried. "How did you know I was here? Selena?"

"She was worried about you. And I sort of begged her. Don't be mad, just please listen. What you think you saw or heard wasn't about me leaving. I told you I'm not leaving you again."

She sat up, and he could see the confusion in her face.

"But it was Tom, and he said you had a deal."

"And we do, but it has nothing to do with me taking another field assignment."

"How can I believe that?"

"Because I'm telling you it's the truth. I said I wasn't going to leave you again. And I'm not."

Then she started sobbing even harder. "Oh, my God. I'm so sorry. I don't know why, but I just assumed… Then I called you a liar…oh, Max."

Max sat on the couch next to her and put his arm around her. She dropped her head onto his shoulder, and the weight of it felt good. Still, it made him sad.

"Why did I jump to a conclusion like that?" she asked, still berating herself. "All this sadness just because—"

"Because you don't really trust me yet," Max said, trying not to let it hurt too much.

Eleanor lifted her head and turned to him. "I…"

He shook his head. She couldn't finish that sentence because it was true.

"I get it, Nor. This is going to have to be a process for us. I didn't just leave you when I took that last assignment. That hurt, but you also thought I left you permanently, and I think that's what you still haven't forgiven me for."

Her face collapsed and more tears came. Max could feel her pain, and it destroyed him, too. He had been separated from her, and hurt. But even through that pain, he knew he would never stop trying to find a way back to her. He had known she was alive.

Nor had thought he was dead. That there was no going back from that, no second chance she was hoping for.

"Losing you was the hardest thing. Only today, when I was going to meet you for lunch, I thought that it felt different. That I wasn't alone anymore. Then I saw you with Tom and jumped to that horrible conclusion—"

"You'll get there, Nor. You'll get to a point

someday when you don't look at me and think I have one foot at the door."

"How do you know?" she wailed. "How do you know I'll get there? That I will trust you deep down to the depth of my soul?"

"Because I'm going to work every second of every day to try and make that happen. All I need is for you to be open to letting me do my thing."

She nodded. "I am trying. I really am. I thought... I thought I was there. I really liked not feeling alone. I liked feeling like I was part of something again. Maybe I was afraid of being that happy. I don't know."

"The fear will go away in time. I know it will. Every morning when you wake up and see my ugly face, you'll start to know it, too."

She touched his face then, and he liked the feel of her fingers over his skin.

"Are you mad that I'm not there, yet? That I jumped to the wrong conclusion so easily?"

"Not mad," he said. And he wasn't. Hurt maybe, but he had to get over that. Their marriage wasn't just about two people who broke up and were now trying to fix things. The wounds and the grief went deeper than that. "We just need time."

"Why are you being so patient with me?"

"Because I love you," he said easily. "Remember?"

She gasped, and he smiled at the sound. Then he moved in to kiss her. Her cheeks were damp, but her lips were soft and welcoming. He sank into her and could feel the hot wet heat of her mouth. He thought this would be good. Making her feel better after having felt so shitty for hours.

He pressed into her body and was delighted to feel the bump of their child pressed against his stomach.

"Pretty soon, your belly is going to get so big, we'll have to find new and creative ways to make love."

"Hmm, what did you have in mind?" she asked, running her hands along his ear, down his neck. Finding those points on his body that she knew would make him shiver with excitement. Nor was the only woman who had truly figured out how to touch him. Because each touch felt like it was more than skin on skin.

It felt like she was touching and stroking his heart, as well.

He turned her then so that her back was to his chest. Then he laid them both on their sides. Suddenly, he felt this urgent need to be inside her. He didn't want to play, he didn't want to tease. He wanted to connect them again, taking another step in repairing the damage that had been done to his wife's heart.

"Take off your leggings," he said gruffly in her ear.

She shivered again, and he knew she, too, was already aroused. Her hands went up her tunic top, and he saw her leggings along with a flash of white cotton that was her panties fly over their heads while he undid his jeans. He freed his cock and positioned her again, pulling her leg over his jean-clad thigh and pushing against her wet folds.

Then he was pushing inside her even as one hand was wrapped on her belly, the other against her breasts, holding her against him. He rocked his hips into hers from behind in a slow and steady rhythm even as he buried his face in her neck.

"Max," she whispered as he felt her body tightening around him.

"Say it again," he demanded. "Say my name again."

"Max."

He thrust harder into her and thought he needed to go even further, even deeper into her. Until there was nothing that would ever separate them again. Then she cried out his name one more time.

"Nor," he cried into her neck, coming hard and deep inside her. "I love you. I love you."

He waited for the words back. Wondered if, in this heady state of pleasure, she might tell him what he knew to be true.

Because the thing was she never would have been as hurt by his death if she hadn't loved him as deeply and as passionately as he did her.

But there was only her panting breaths as she came down from the high, only the soft beat of her heart under his hand.

Patience, he thought. She just needed more time.

ELEANOR WOKE TO the smell of coffee. She and Max had made their way from the couch to the bedroom where he had made love to her yet again. This time slower and more leisurely. As if they had all the time in the world.

It had been delicious.

An escape from the reality of their marriage, her company and everything else. She knew Max was right. She obviously didn't completely believe in him yet, but he had such faith that she eventually would, she decided to go along with it.

She still couldn't say the words. The words she was sure he had wanted to hear. Back when they were married, Max used to tell her all the time that he loved her, and every time he did, she repeated the sentiment. Because it was her truth. He loved her and she loved him.

She still believed it was her truth, but she knew it wouldn't be fair to give him those words without all of her trust, as well.

Time, he'd said. She just needed more time.

She got up from the bed, took a shower and put her tunic from yesterday back on. She obviously hadn't thought to pack when she decided to come up here, so she would have to make it home in day-old panties.

Panties that she realized were on the floor in

the living room somewhere. Then she saw they were folded on a chair in the bedroom on top of her leggings. Why the thought of Max taking the time to pick up and fold her clothes seemed so sweet, she didn't know. She joined him in the kitchen and he poured her a cup of coffee.

"Just half a cup," she reminded him. "Trying to keep the caffeine to a minimum."

"How do you feel?"

Eleanor thought about that. She hadn't felt nauseous at all this morning. "Good," she said. "Really good. Must be this whole second trimester thing kicking in."

"Well if you get even hornier in this second trimester than in the first one, I guess I'll have to work that much harder at being your sex slave. It's a tough job, but someone has to do it."

She laughed, but now that she thought about, she did still feel a little turned on. Whether that was a carryover from last night, she didn't know. She was about to mention it when he changed the subject to something much less sexy.

"So, in an effort to work on you trusting me, why don't you tell me about your meeting with Daniel yesterday."

Then it all came back. His threat, the fact that he wanted even more now. And the surety that there was a mole in her company feeding information to Daniel. About her business, which stung, but also about her baby, and that really pissed her off.

The harsh reality of the world, which had seemed miles away last night, was suddenly all right there.

"I was going to tell you at lunch."

"I'm not going to lie. I'm little upset you didn't think to tell me before you met with him."

Eleanor squirmed on the stool she sat on, even as she sipped on her coffee to bide more time. "I guess I didn't know what you would think. If you would be happy because it would mean me spending less time at work. Or angry that I wasn't willing to fight to hold on to the thing that I had built. I felt like it had to be my call, so, no matter what, I wouldn't resent you. Can you understand that?"

"Yes," he said. "But you need to know I would have been behind whatever decision you had reached. I want what you want. If that's the company and I have to work around your schedule, so be it. If you are ready to let it go, then I'll support that, too."

Eleanor frowned. "Even if I was willing to let it go, I'm not now. Daniel the Douchebag changed the offer. Now he wants controlling interest. That's not going to happen."

"That dick."

Eleanor sighed. "He says it's just business, but I can't help think there is an element of revenge in it for him. Daniel is a man who is used to getting what he wants. And as courteous and polite as he was about the whole situation between us, I think he resents the fact that I broke things off with him. He's not used to losing...anything."

"So he's taking your company in retaliation? That just makes him a sore loser in my opinion. The good news is we have options."

"What do you mean by options?"

"Your problem was that you were overextended and couldn't pay your contractors—"

"Max," she said warily. "What did you do?"

He smiled, but to Eleanor, it looked more ruthless than happy.

"I made a deal." He wiggled his eyebrows, and she couldn't help it, she laughed.

"I CAN'T BELIEVE you did this," she whispered as they sat in the waiting area outside Daniel's office.

They had driven separately to Denver, and Max had encouraged her to call Daniel and make the appointment for the next day.

Now they were sitting together waiting for him. The appointment had been set for two o'clock, and it was fifteen past the hour. Either Daniel was doing it deliberately as a power play, or he was legitimately running late as his assistant had suggested.

"I didn't do anything other than give you a choice. In the end you are the one who made the call."

He took her hand and squeezed it, and it felt amazing. Max had her back. Max was letting her choose what she wanted to do. Max was making it possible for her to have everything.

"I still can't believe it."

"Believe it," he said. "I love you."

The words again. Always the words. Offered so easily and so freely. Sometimes she wondered if his endless patience would run out one day. She hoped not. She really hoped not. Because she did believe he was right. That all she needed was more time.

"Eleanor!" Daniel said as the door to his office opened. "Welcome back. And I see you brought reinforcements."

She could practically hear Max growling behind her as they both stood.

"Daniel," she said. "If you have a minute."

"Of course," he replied. He stepped into his office.

Eleanor turned to Max. "This shouldn't take long," she said.

"You're sure you don't want me in there?"

She shook her head. "It was enough that you were here with me. I've got all the support I need."

"I'll be waiting."

Eleanor made her way into Daniel's office. She didn't bother to sit. This time she was wearing one of the maternity dresses she'd bought only yesterday after she and Max returned to Denver.

She placed her hand on her belly and wondered for the one thousandth time if she was doing the right thing. Not just for her, or the company, but for her baby, too. Then she thought about what it would mean to have a baby girl and to show that girl that she could do anything she wanted in life. That no dream was too big to handle.

"I'll make it quick, Daniel. I will not be accepting your offer."

He sat behind his desk, his fingers pressed together in a steeple. "That's unfortunate. I assume it was my request for controlling interest?"

"It was your request for any of it, really. Head to Toe is mine. I built it, and I'm going to be the person to grow it into something bigger."

He frowned then, as if she'd said something naive. "You understand you've got that little problem with your cash flow."

"That isn't a problem any longer. I've had another investor step up, and I've chosen to accept his offer."

"Another investor?"

"Yes, it seems because of the negligence of the ship's captain to not turn around and avoid the storm, a settlement was made to the research foundation. As the sole survivor of that storm, the settlement belongs to Max. My new partner in Head to Toe."

Daniel flinched. "I see."

"No, I don't think you do see," Eleanor said tightly. "I'm not sure if you were responsible for my technical difficulties last week or not, but I know you have someone inside my company providing you with information. I would imagine the only incentive a person might have for doing that would be money. With the influx of cash from Max's settlement, I'll be hiring a private investigator to do a more thorough background check and investigation into each and every one of my employees. I'll find whoever tipped you off. So you can either tell that person to quit now, or prepare to be fired later. My company's business is no longer your business. Are we clear?"

"I could create a competing company," Daniel said, neither admitting to nor acknowledging his mole's behavior.

Eleanor smiled. "Bring it. Nothing like a little competition to get the blood stirred. And I've got a pretty big head start on you, so good luck trying catch up. But you're certainly free to try."

Daniel stood then, and put his hands in his pockets. Eleanor couldn't say he looked defeated, but he did look resigned, and she thought that might be just as good.

"You, too. Good luck…with everything," he said.

Then he sat again and turned to his computer. It was clear to see she was dismissed. Eleanor Harper may be the only woman to have ever survived Daniel the corporate shark and lived to tell the tale.

She walked out of the office, and Max stood. She smiled at him and gave him a thumbs-up.

"You tell the asshole off?"

"I told him I wasn't accepting his offer. That I had another partner I much preferred working with."

Max put an arm around her shoulders and brought her in tight to his body. "Who would have thought I would be a part of a fashion company?"

Eleanor laughed. "Nobody. Nobody would have ever thought that you would be part of a fashion company."

"I might have to start stepping up my game."

Eleanor considered that. Getting to dress Max up. "That is definitely something we can fix."

"We?"

"Oh, you are in for it now, Max Harper. You are about to put your fate and your wardrobe into the hands of the most ruthless fashionista of all… Selena."

"Why are you making me feel like I should be afraid?"

Eleanor rubbed her hands together. "Be afraid, Max. Be very afraid. You are about to get a first-class makeover."

Max stopped then, and turned to her, lifting her chin with his finger so that her eyes were pinned to his.

"Promise me this," he said quietly. "If I let Selena work me over today, you'll work me over tonight."

Eleanor knew a good deal when she heard one. "Done."

CHAPTER TWENTY-ONE

ALLIE ROCKED BACK and forth on her feet. "Not sure why he's late," she said to the people currently standing in her living room. "He's usually home by now."

"We're in no hurry," Maggie, who worked at the town hall, said.

Allie smiled. "Thanks. I know I must seem nervous."

"Any bride would be," Maggie replied.

Allie sucked in her breath. Right. Because this was it. This was the big day. Even if Mike didn't know it yet.

Then she heard a car pull up, and her nerves nearly exploded. What if he didn't like her idea? What if she ruined everything by doing this? What if he got angry? Despite being mortified, she knew she would be crushed.

This was a big deal. This was her taking a risk and doing the thing that Mike said she needed to do. She was trying to prove to him that she was strong enough to be a woman he could love. A woman he deserved.

"Allie? Whose car is that out back?"

"I'm in the living room," Allie called. Then she wrapped her hands around the bouquet of wild flowers she had picked out. Because they were her favorite. Just like the simple, white dress she had chosen. Miles away from what had been picked out for her to wear. Her hair was down and soft around her shoulders. She had just a hint of makeup on and splash of Mike's favorite scent on her. So that when he saw her, he would know it was her. Not just someone who looked like a fancy version of her.

Tucked in the flowers was the paper with her vows. It probably wasn't fair not to give Mike a chance to write his own, but she knew he would have hated that kind of thing anyway. He wasn't one for flowery words or sappy emotions. He would much prefer to say "I do" a few times and call himself married.

But she knew she needed to say more.

"Allie?" he said as he came into the living room. "What is this?"

She'd strung Christmas lights around the

room. All blue. She'd lit a fire in the fireplace because that added a different color element. She was standing in front of Judge Martin and Maggie, who worked as his clerk at the town hall.

"Our marriage license was approved. Which means we can get married any time after that."

"Yeah. I thought that's what we were doing in three months?"

"We're going to. The whole show and everything. With the fancy dress and the bridesmaids and groomsmen and our families there and everything. But you told me you wanted me to stand up for what I wanted. Well, I want this. I want just us to be married together. I don't want to share the day with everyone. I don't want to wait. I want this day to be ours and ours alone. I guess I'm surprising you with your own wedding." She bit her bottom lip then. "What do you think?"

She held her breath, then watched as a huge grin took up his whole face. "You want this?"

"Yep."

"And you're telling me this is going to happen right here and right now because it's what would make you happy?"

Allie nodded.

"Okay, then. Let's get hitched."

Mike took her hand, and together they stood in front of Judge Martin with Maggie as their witness.

Judge Martin did the normal vows for Mike.

Did he take Allie to be his wife?

He did.

Did he take her in sickness and in health, for richer or poorer, so long as they both shall live?

He did.

Then Judge Martin turned to her, and she gulped. She had the piece of paper, but she didn't need to take it out. She knew the words by heart.

"Mike, you know I love you. That's never been in doubt. Hardly from the moment we met. But what you didn't know is how I struggled to be worthy of you."

"Allie..."

"No," she said. "No interrupting my vows. I did. I wanted to be worthy of you. Because you're not like any man I've ever known. Not only are you kind and patient, but you always want what's best for me. You push me to be a better person, and because I love you, I accept that challenge. I take you to be my husband, for richer or poorer, in sickness and in health for as long we both shall live. Today, because that's what *I* want."

He smiled and leaned in to kiss her.

"You're supposed to wait until I say it's okay," Judge Martin reminded him with a chuckle.

"Oh. Sorry." But then Mike kissed her anyway.

"You may now continue to kiss the bride."

Maggie sniffled and clapped her hands.

Allie pulled back from Mike and thanked her visitors. "Now remember what we agreed upon? No one breathes a word of this to my mother."

Maggie slid her fingers over her lips as if she was zipping them shut.

"Not a word," Judge Martin agreed.

"Okay. Then it's time for champagne!"

Three months later

"STOP FUSSING," MARILYN SAID, even as Eleanor tried to remain still. She was seated in a chair in the vestibule of the church where the wedding was to take place in a little less than an hour while her mother added more hair pins to keep her hair in place on top of her head.

"Seriously, Mom. How many pins does a person need to hold an updo?"

"If my count is correct," Allie chimed in, "one million and two."

Marilyn harrumphed. "That sounds about right."

"Besides, it's not as if anyone is going to be looking at me, anyway. All eyes are going to be on Allie. She's the bride."

"I don't know, Eleanor. You're basically as big as a whale. It might be hard for people to see me at all if I'm standing next to you."

Eleanor glowered and reached over to pinch her sister.

"Stop that," Marilyn chastised her. "No red marks on her arm before she walks down the aisle."

"Yeah, Eleanor. I'm the bride, remember." Allie stuck her tongue out at her sister.

"How is it that you are so relaxed?" Eleanor wanted to know. Her mother had been her usual self. Fussing and prodding and trying to make everything exactly perfect. Allie had been completely unaffected by it. She'd simply gone along with every request and order as if none of it was stressful at all. As if today wasn't the single biggest day of her life.

Allie smiled and shrugged. "Don't know. Just feel pretty chill about it all, really."

Eleanor was anything but chill. She felt full and bloated and about ready to explode. She knew she was sweating through her purple maternity gown, which Marilyn said made her look elegant and statuesque, but she thought made her look like a giant eggplant.

Plus there was the cramping.

She'd been having Braxton Hicks contractions for the past few weeks. At her last doctor's appointment she was still only a centimeter dilated, though. The doctor had said it could happen any day, or it could be another week or two.

Babies, it seemed, had their own timetable.

But she was feeling strange today. Like her whole body was getting ready for something big.

I love you, little baby, but please hold off until after the ceremony.

Eleanor rubbed her belly, mentally trying to convey the words. Maybe she should go find Max. Tell him about the contractions and that he should start to time them. But if she did that, then he would probably freak out and want to take her to the hospital right away.

She was not going to miss Allie's wedding. Surely, if she was going into labor, then she could spare an hour to see her little sister get married.

"Okay. You both look as good as you can look," Marilyn proclaimed.

Eleanor and Allie shared a smile. It was their mother's idea of a compliment.

"Now let's get this show on the road." Marilyn walked over to the vestibule door, opened it and made a signal.

The organist must have been waiting for it, because immediately the music started up.

Allie had decided she wanted to be given away by both her mother and her sister. At first, Marilyn balked at the break of tradition, but on this decision Allie would not be moved.

And so that was how it happened. Allie was in the middle with Mom on her right arm and Eleanor on her left arm. They made it exactly halfway down the aisle when Eleanor felt the rush of wetness between her legs.

She stopped, and because her arm was

linked with Allie's, Allie and her mother had to stop, too.

"What's happening?" Marilyn asked. "Why are we stopping?"

"Oh, no," Eleanor said just as a major wave of pain rolled over her belly.

"Eleanor?" Allie asked.

"My water broke."

"Oh, shit." Allie laughed. "That is hilarious."

Not really. Elcanor didn't find a single thing funny about the pain.

Max made his way up the aisle with Mike following closely behind him. The whole church was on their feet and staring in disbelief.

"Nor?" Max said, reaching her first.

"It's happening," she panted, even as the contraction started to recede. "Like now."

"Let's go!" Allie said.

"Go? We can't go. You have to get married," Marilyn shouted.

"Oh, Mom, don't worry about that. Mike and I got married months ago. This was just for show."

Eleanor's eyes popped wide as she stared at her sister. "Are you kidding me?"

Allie smiled smugly even as she took Mike's hand. "It's what I wanted."

"Allison Ann Harper."

"Davies, Mom. Allison Ann Davies."

Marilyn put a hand to her chest. "This is a disaster."

"Uh, I can appreciate you're upset, Marilyn, but I sort of would like to get my wife to the hospital," Max said.

Eleanor was in agreement with that as another contraction rolled over her. That seemed really fast. "Oh, man, this hurts."

"You doing okay?" Max asked her.

And suddenly it all made such crazy sense. Eleanor laughed through the pain even as she doubled over. "I want a wedding!"

"What?" Max asked.

"I want a big wedding. I want the church and my own dress and the party."

"Seriously, Nor? Can we talk about this later? Like after you have the kid?"

Eleanor reached and grabbed Max's hand. For months, he'd done nothing but be the most supportive and most amazing husband a wife could imagine. He'd been there for her every step as she grew the business. He'd told her he loved her all the time without ever pressing her for more. He'd given her the time she had needed to finally heal. And it was now, standing in the aisle of a church wearing her hideous purple dress with a puddle between her legs, she knew in her heart that she had done just that.

"Max Harper, I love you. Will you marry me again and give me a big, splashy wedding with all the trimmings so that everyone will know how much I love you?"

She could see the tears in his eyes. Because he knew, more than anyone, what her declaration meant. It meant not only that she had not only overcome the grief of losing him, but it also meant she trusted him. One hundred percent trusted him.

"Yes, Eleanor Harper. I will marry you and give you everything you have ever wanted. I promise."

He kissed her then, and she held on to him with everything she had.

"This is so sweet," Allie said.

"Sweet? This is supposed to be your wedding!"

Allie patted Marilyn on the back. "Look at

it this way, Mom. At least you're going to get another shot at it."

Max pulled away from Eleanor. "Can we please go to the hospital now?"

"Yes," Eleanor agreed. "Let's go have a baby!"

At that, the entire church of family and friends erupted into applause.

Seven hours later

"SHE'S SO TINY. I can't get over how tiny she is," Allie said, looking down at the bundle in her arms.

Eleanor leaned back in the bed with a contented smile. The word *labor* was no joke. Bringing Sarah Allison into this world had been a rough job, but it was done now and Eleanor was pleased with her efforts.

"I want her back," she said, and her sister quickly handed her over.

Baby nestled in her arms, everything felt right again.

Then the hospital door opened, and Max entered with bags full of food. With everything that had happened, no one had eaten a thing that day. All their family and friends had gone on with the reception. Allie and Mike had told everyone to have a good time without them.

But then they had come to the hospital with Marilyn to sit and wait.

Now everyone was happy and starving.

Max handed off the bags to Mike to distribute, then he carefully sat on the bed to gaze into his daughter's tiny face.

"I missed her when I was gone," he whispered.

"You were gone for less than half an hour," she pointed out.

"Yes, and that was too long," he said. "Can I hold her again?"

Eleanor decided she couldn't hog all the baby time, so she handed her daughter off to her father.

Looking at Max holding their daughter, she realized what a miracle life really was.

When he'd died, she'd died. Now there was nothing but life.

"I love you, Max." She promised herself then she would say it every day to him from now until her last.

"I love you, too. But I'm not giving her back just yet."

And Eleanor thought that was okay. For now.

* * * * *

*If you enjoyed this Superromance book
by Stephanie Doyle,
she has a wonderful backlist
of romances including
HER SECRET SERVICE AGENT,
THE COMEBACK OF ROY WALKER,
SCOUT'S HONOR and
BETTING ON THE ROOKIE.*

*Available at Harlequin.com or
for online order at retailers
where Harlequin books are sold.*

Get 2 Free Books,
Plus 2 Free Gifts—
just for trying the Reader Service!

HRLP17R3

Get 2 Free Books,
Plus 2 Free Gifts—
just for trying the Reader Service!

Get 2 Free Books,
Plus 2 Free Gifts—
just for trying the Reader Service!

READERSERVICE.COM

Manage your account online!

- Review your order history
- Manage your payments
- Update your address

> *We've designed the*
> *Reader Service website*
> *just for you.*

Enjoy all the features!

- Discover new series available to you, and read excerpts from any series.
- Respond to mailings and special monthly offers.
- Browse the Bonus Bucks catalog and online-only exculsives.
- Share your feedback.

Visit us at:
ReaderService.com